Cowboy Versus Samurai

by Michael Golamco

Inspired by "Cyrano De Bergerac"
by Edmond Rostand

A SAMUEL FRENCH ACTING EDITION

NEW YORK HOLLYWOOD LONDON TORONTO

SAMUELFRENCH.COM

ISBN 978-0-573-69940-5 Printed in U.S.A. #29757

MUSIC USE NOTE

Licensees are solely responsible for obtaining formal written permission from copyright owners to use copyrighted music in the performance of this play and are strongly cautioned to do so. If no such permission is obtained by the licensee, then the licensee must use only original music that the licensee owns and controls. Licensees are solely responsible and liable for all music clearances and shall indemnify the copyright owners of the play and their licensing agent, Samuel French, Inc., against any costs, expenses, losses and liabilities arising from the use of music by licensees.

IMPORTANT BILLING AND CREDIT REQUIREMENTS

All producers of *COWBOY VERSUS SAMURAI* *must* give credit to the Author of the Play in all programs distributed in connection with performances of the Play, and in all instances in which the title of the Play appears for the purposes of advertising, publicizing or otherwise exploiting the Play and/or a production. The name of the Author *must* appear on a separate line on which no other name appears, immediately following the title and *must* appear in size of type not less than fifty percent of the size of the title type.

COWBOY VERSUS SAMURAI was first produced by NAATCO (National Asian American Theatre Company, Mia Katigbak, Artistic Producing Director) at the Rattlestick Theatre in New York City in November, 2005. The production was directed by Lloyd Suh, with sets by Sarah Lambert, with lights by Stepehen Petrilli, music and sound design by Robert Murphy, fight choreography by Qui Nguyen, and costumes by Elly van Home. The production stage manager was Karen Hergesheimer. The cast was as follows:

DEL .... Timothy Davis

TRAVIS .... Joel de la Fuente

CHESTER .... C.S. Lee

VERONICA .... Hana Moon

CHARACTERS

DEL

TRAVIS

CHESTER

VERONICA

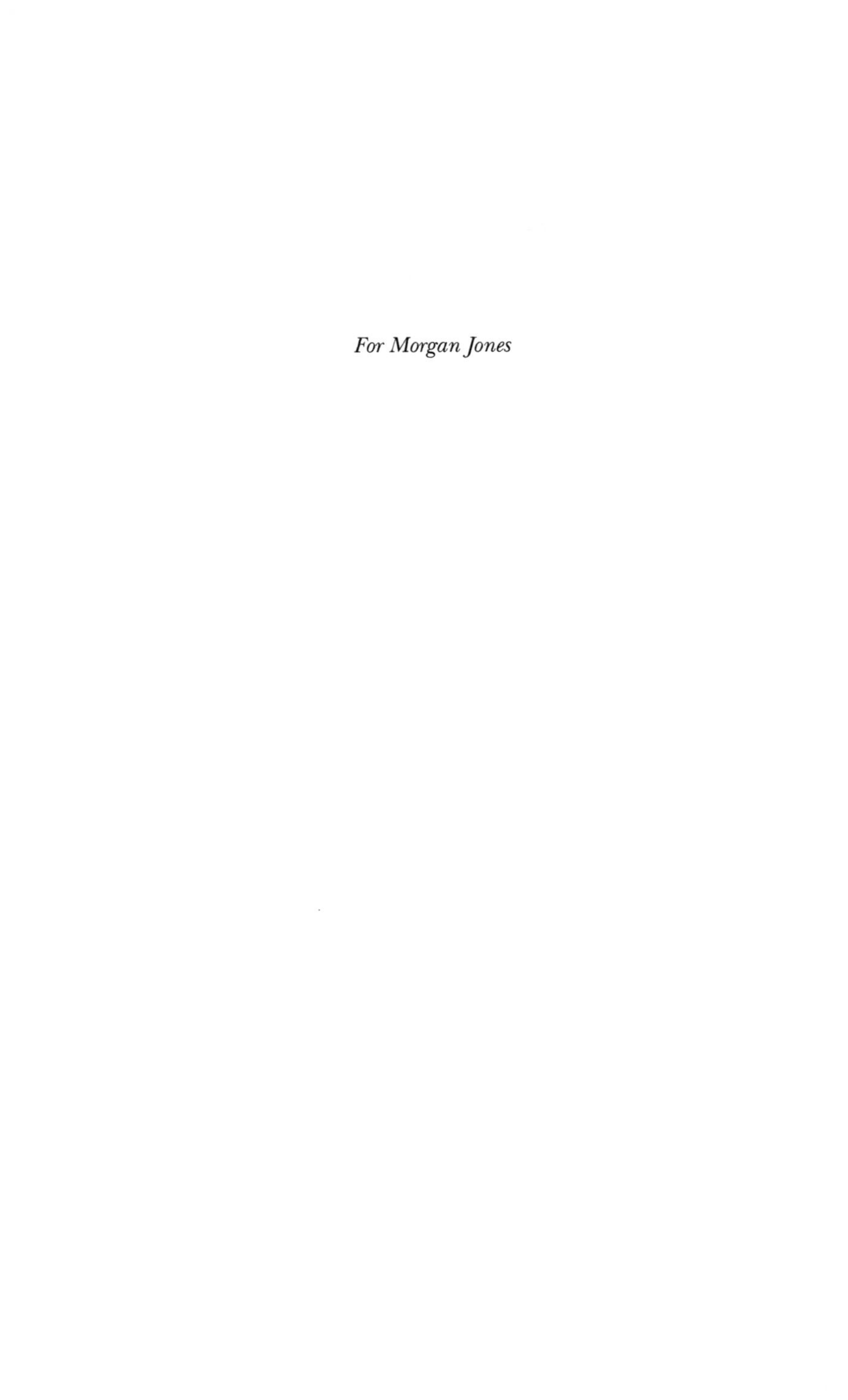

For Morgan Jones

ACT ONE

Scene One

(Breakneck, Wyoming. Population: One thousand. Present day.)

(Outdoors. Sound of the wind.)

*(***DEL***, late twenties/early thirties, Caucasian, on the left. He is ruggedly handsome, an All-American Cowboy.)*

(He addresses us directly:)

(Letter #1:)

DEL. Things in nature always hide. Lizards change the color of their skins. Moths live or die based on the color of their wings. They do these things because when you stand out in the world you invite danger. You will be caught by unseen teeth. You will be eaten alive by something that was waiting for you to show yourself.

And that's how I felt, standing like a shadow on your outskirts, invisible.

But with this letter, I throw away my fear. For you I am a bright green frog blazing on a lily pad. I am a million tropical birds roaring into the sky. I am a bee dancing across honeycombs; I am a baboon's blossoming ass.

And I suppose that's love. It wants to be heard. It needs to be heard. So please: Hear me out.

(fade)

Scene Two

(A small-town high school classroom.)

*(***TRAVIS PARK***, late twenties/early thirties, Korean American, sits alone in one of the student desk chairs.)*

(He's doodling on a piece of paper.)

*(***CHESTER***, 20s-30s, Asian American of Unknown Origin, stands at a teacher's desk. He is possibly dressed in black military fatigues, Che Guevarran.)*

(He bangs a gavel –)

CHESTER. Order! As President of the Breakneck Asian American Alliance, I call this meeting to order! Will the Secretary rise and read the minutes from our last meeting?

*(***TRAVIS*** stands, flips the piece of paper over and reads off of it –)*

TRAVIS. Last week we discussed the fact that Shelby's Grocery Store doesn't carry tofu. Then we discussed boycotting Shelby's Grocery Store. Then our President attempted to find a method for ordering tofu through the Internet...and then the Secretary called the President a moron.

CHESTER. Moving on –

TRAVIS. And then we voted on whether the President actually is a moron, which ended in a tie –

CHESTER. Yes, MOVING ON. Our first order of business is –

*(***TRAVIS*** raises his hand –)*

Yes.

TRAVIS. I move that we change our regular meeting place to Heck's Tavern.

CHESTER. Anyone second that motion?

*(***TRAVIS*** sighs and raises his hand again.)*

All right, let's bring it to a vote. All in favor, say "AYE."

TRAVIS. Aye.

CHESTER. All opposed say "NAY." Nay. All right, we have a tie. In which case, the bylaws of BAAA state that the President must make a final decision…and his decision is: NO.

TRAVIS. Oh, come on, Chester! If I have to come to these stupid meetings I want to be able to drink a beer.

CHESTER. In order to preserve BAAA's integrity, BAAA must maintain meeting locations that do not serve alcohol.

TRAVIS. Would you quit saying "BAAA"? You sound like a militant sheep.

CHESTER. I am anything but sheep-like, my brother. The Asian Man must stand for dignity and righteousness – not getting red-in-the-face while he falls off a bar stool.

TRAVIS. These meetings are a joke. You and I are the only Asian people in town.

CHESTER. Which is why we must maintain solidarity, my Korean Brother. Solidarity in the face of constant and deliberate oppression. Shelby's Grocery Store: An openly racist seller of Occidental-only foodstuffs.

TRAVIS. Mr. Shelby has said, repeatedly, that he won't carry anything that only two people are going to buy.

CHESTER. Solidarity. Heck's Tavern: Center of Foreign and Domestic Imperialism, what with its so-called selection of "Import Beer." Where's my Tsing-Tao? My Kirin Ichiban? Can I get a fuckin' Hite?

TRAVIS. I thought you weren't into getting red-faced and falling off bar stools.

CHESTER. Well, I might be if I could get a glass of something from the Motherland. See, Travis, one voice alone accomplishes nothing. And that's why BAAA exists – to give us more than one voice.

TRAVIS. Two voices.

CHESTER. That's right: Two Strong Asian American voices. And if you and I stick together, we can affect some change in this shitty little town.

TRAVIS. But you see Chester, I like this shitty little town. I like the fact that Heck hasn't changed his tavern since 1973. I like –

CHESTER. Well –

TRAVIS. Shut up. I like bowling in a two-lane alley that's connected to an Episcopal Church. I like flipping through the library's *National Geographics* with all the aboriginal titties snipped out. I like all of these things because I enjoy certain charms. The charms, if you will, of small town life. And I know you grew up here, but these things are still new to me.

CHESTER. If I had a car and some money, I'd be sipping iced green tea on a beach. But that's okay. Don't lift a finger, remain seated in your little Caucasian corner. I will handle this weeks' business by myself: The BAAA membership drive.

TRAVIS. Membership drive?

CHESTER. Yes. There's a potential new member moving into town. Last name Lee.

TRAVIS. There are plenty of Lees that aren't Asian. Christopher Lee. Tommy Lee Jones. Lee Majors.

CHESTER. From New York.

TRAVIS. Spike Lee.

CHESTER. From Flushing, Queens.

TRAVIS. Flushing what?

CHESTER. You're from California, so you wouldn't understand. Flushing, Queens is the Korean capital of New York City. And it gets better: Last name Lee, first name Veronica.

(deliciously)

Korean Veronica Lee.

TRAVIS. Leave her alone, Chester. Keep your crazy militant shit to yourself.

CHESTER. No way fella. It's bad enough living in this two-donkey town. I'm an island of yellow in a sea of white.

TRAVIS. It's like someone took a piss in the snow.

CHESTER. We are going to embrace this hopefully-lovely Korean Sister with open arms and show her that Asian America thrives in Breakneck, Wyoming. You actually have another thing in common with her: She's also a teacher.

TRAVIS. Wonderful. Now we know you won't be able to hypnotize her into drinking your Kool-Aid.

CHESTER. You always belittle my ideas, Travis. Why is that?

TRAVIS. It's because your ideas are stupid, Chester. If you tell her your conspiracy theory that American rice contains penis-shrinking chemicals, I'm walking out.

CHESTER. I am upholding our identity, my brother. For within that identity lies our dignity.

TRAVIS. Fine. But give it a rest sometime, okay? Support some other causes. Save the Whales. Stop deforestation. Become a Nazi or something.

(as he exits –)

And one more thing – next time I'm going to be at Heck's Tavern, with or without you. I might even start my own club. The Breakneck Travis American Alliance. That's B-TAAH to you. B-TAAH! Anyone who wants to drink beer with me is in. Make it the Breakneck Beer American Alliance. Buh-buh-Ahh! Buh-buh-Ahh!

*(**TRAVIS** exits.)*

*(**CHESTER** in prayer:)*

CHESTER. O Bruce, please show Travis the error of his ways. He's a good guy, even if he is a race traitor. Oh, and by the way, please make sure that Veronica Lee is hot. Hot-and-buttered. Shie-shie, O Great One.

(He bows.)

Scene Three

(The classroom, a few days later.)

*(***VERONICA LEE***, late twenties/early thirties, Korean American, sits at the teachers' desk. She's beautiful, glasses-wearing.)*

(She riffles through a cardboard box as **CHESTER** *paces around, lecturing –)*

CHESTER. SD-3. Remember that name.

VERONICA. SD-3. Right.

CHESTER. Yes. It was created by scientists under the Truman administration. And it's been proven – PROVEN – that SD-3 can be found in all commercially available rice in America. How does it get there? Hmm? Do you know?

VERONICA. You're going to tell me, aren't you?

CHESTER. The GOVERNMENT sprays it onto every single grain of –

*(***TRAVIS*** enters, surprised to see them.)*

TRAVIS. Hello.

CHESTER. Hello, Travis. Have you met Veronica Lee?

TRAVIS. *(handshake)* Hi, I'm Travis Park.

VERONICA. Hello Travis Park.

CHESTER. I was just telling Veronica here all about SD-3.

TRAVIS. Right, SD-3.

(beat)

Chester, aren't you late for your shift?

CHESTER. What?

(checks his watch)

Oh damn, you're correct.

(to **VERONICA***)*

I'm the assistant manager of the only ethnic restaurant in town.

TRAVIS. Taco Tuesday.

CHESTER. *(grumbles)* Yes, Taco Tuesday.

VERONICA. I used to live right next to a Taco Tuesday. I'm a fan.

CHESTER. What a marvelous coincidence. You know, before I met you, I was drowning in the snide irony of being an Asian Man working in a Mexican fast-food restaurant. But now –

VERONICA. You're late.

CHESTER. I'm late.

*(**CHESTER** hands her a flyer.)*

We have a meeting this Wednesday at 8PM, right here in Travis's – I mean, yours and Travis's – classroom.

VERONICA. I'll see if I can make it.

CHESTER. That's all I ask. Stay strong.

*(as **CHESTER** walks out –)*

Thank-you-Bruce!

*(**CHESTER** exits.)*

*(**VERONICA** shows the flyer to **TRAVIS** with a puzzled smile.)*

TRAVIS. It's not his fault. He doesn't know what he is.

VERONICA. Somebody should let him know that he's kind of a creep.

TRAVIS. No, I mean he literally doesn't know what he is. He was adopted. And when his parents picked him up from the airport, they forgot to ask the adoption people which country he came from.

VERONICA. You're kidding.

TRAVIS. No, I'm not. And the organization that brought him here went out of business so…he never found out what kind of Asian he is. Don't worry – he's harmless. He's just a little confused.

(She starts to unpack a cardboard box.)

So you're Veronica Lee from New York City.

VERONICA. That's right, Hoss.

TRAVIS. You've got the cowboy slang down. That's good.

VERONICA. That's my backup in case this teaching gig doesn't work out.

TRAVIS. So what are you doing in Wyoming?

VERONICA. I'm in this program that puts teachers where they're desperately needed.

TRAVIS. Well, that's us, I guess. Desperate. We have graduating seniors who still like to eat paste.

VERONICA. They give you your choice of places, so I'm just here for a couple of semesters to try it out.

TRAVIS. Just to try it out?

VERONICA. Yeah. I've always wanted to live in a place that has a band that sounds like the Country Bear Jamboree.

TRAVIS. There's this bar in town that has a band that plays Beatles songs with a washboard and a jug.

VERONICA. That sounds perfect.

TRAVIS. So what are you teaching?

VERONICA. Biology. I cut open dead animals and show the insides to kids.

TRAVIS. That's great. Do you do that at parties?

VERONICA. You're an English teacher, aren't you?

TRAVIS. How'd you figure that out?

VERONICA. You don't have many weird quirks, so science is out. You are clearly not a math teacher. You look too sober to teach art, and history…not history. So you must be an English teacher.

TRAVIS. That's amazing.

VERONICA. Plus, I was looking through your desk and I found all these essays on Huckleberry Finn.

TRAVIS. Please help yourself to anything else you find in there.

VERONICA. Thanks. So what are the kids like?

TRAVIS. Well, all of the county filters into this school so we get a lot ranchers' kids. They're great for the most part. Except for Bobby Sorenson. He keeps making chinky-eyes at me.

VERONICA. You're kidding. I met Bobby Sorenson. He's a sweetheart.

TRAVIS. You have the advantage of being a beautiful woman. I'm just another jerk in a tie. He keeps asking me if I put pee-pee in his coke. And one of these days, I swear – I'm gonna do it.

(She picks up the empty box.)

VERONICA. It was good to meet you, Travis. Now if you'll excuse me, I've got to go home and tend to a sick cat with no tail.

TRAVIS. Sure.

(beat)

Hey, so I know you've gotten a lot of offers – "If you need anythings"…But if you do need anything –

VERONICA. Like what?

TRAVIS. *Staples,* or glue… They're in the desk –

VERONICA. Uh-huh.

TRAVIS. Or if you're a bulgogi fan, I think it's safe to say that I make the best bulgogi in the entire state of Wyoming.

VERONICA. Not anymore. Now that I'm here.

TRAVIS. You wanna bet?

VERONICA. You know Dr. Peters and his wife? They have the ranch with all the –

TRAVIS & VERONICA. *(together)* White horses –

VERONICA. Yeah. I'm renting the cottage at the end of their road. So if you've got a free evening, I suggest you bring over your bulgogi and we'll see what's up.

TRAVIS. I will.

VERONICA. See you soon, Mr. Park. And get ready to be number two.

(She exits.)

(Lights dim on the classroom as **TRAVIS** *crosses over to* **CHESTER**, *who stands on the side, disappointed.)*

(He's wearing a billowy yellow robe.)

CHESTER. You didn't come to the meeting.

TRAVIS. I'm sorry, Chester. I was busy fixing my roof.

CHESTER. Neither did Veronica Lee.

TRAVIS. She's probably still settling in. When you move into a town full of strangers there are a lot of things you need to take care of.

*(**CHESTER** looks away, defeated –)*

CHESTER. I'll tell you what, Travis: She's yours. You have my blessing. I give her to you.

TRAVIS. What the hell are you talking about?

CHESTER. No, I insist. I've been a monk this long, I can keep on going.

TRAVIS. Don't do me any favors, Chester. Maybe she's looking for an anarchist-militant-psychopath like yourself.

CHESTER. No, I give up. You two were meant to be together. You're both teachers, you're both Korean.

TRAVIS. Sure, we'll be right next the kangaroos on Noah's Ark. Look – there's no guarantee that I'm going to be attracted to her just because she's Asian.

CHESTER. I don't see you mackin' on the Mackenzie Twins.

TRAVIS. That's because I'm not attracted to the Mackenzie Twins.

CHESTER. Me either. Though they are gorgeous, they're still Caucasian She-Devils. But Veronica Lee – her Ying smooths neatly together with our Yang.

TRAVIS. Listen to me carefully: Race has nothing to do with being attracted to someone.

CHESTER. Of course it does, my brother! How are you, an Asian Man, supposed to replicate yourself without the assistance of an Asian Woman? Bruce sent you this Angel on a cloud, and you don't even want to give her a chance.

TRAVIS. Okay, what's up with the Bruce Lee-as-God thing? I was letting everything else slide, but the action-hero-religification is beginning to worry me.

CHESTER. The Asian Man worships who he chooses. So logic dictates that he worship the Supreme Asian Man. And besides, I'm pretty sure I'm Chinese.

TRAVIS. You're not Chinese.

CHESTER. Yes I am.

TRAVIS. What makes you so sure?

CHESTER. I've been studying Mandarin and the words just roll off my tongue. Plus it explains why I'm so darned stingy with my money.

TRAVIS. Fine. "*Gong Xi Fa Cai.*"

CHESTER. What does that mean?

TRAVIS. "I'm glad you're Chinese."

CHESTER. Oh. Thanks!

(beat)

I'd continue chatting with you some more, but I have another meeting to attend.

TRAVIS. *(Re: Chester's yellow robe)* You got choir practice or something?

*(**CHESTER** pulls on a hood, completing his costume: The robes of a Knight of the Ku Klux Klan.)*

TRAVIS. *(aghast)* What the hell are you doing in that?

CHESTER. Undercover research. I'm learning a lot of organizational things. And if you replace the words "White" with "Yellow," and "Aryan" with "Asian," they pretty much say the same things I do at our BAAA meetings. Plus these guys can fry a turkey like you wouldn't believe.

TRAVIS. You're crazy.

CHESTER. And dangerous. But that's how a true Revolutionary has to live. Besides, it's not that tough. All I have to do is eat and drink through these little eye-holes.

(beat)

And now before I depart, here's a pearl of wisdom, my Brother: Give Veronica Lee a chance. Who knows? You may end up banging her.

*(**CHESTER** raises a fist.)*

(fade)

Scene Four

(**DEL** *stands at center wearing a baseball glove.)*

(He kneads the palm of his glove, then addresses us directly:)

(Letter #2:)

DEL. My Uncle Pinky had three ears. Two normal ears and a tiny little ear behind his left one. It was about the size of a nickel. He used to cover up his regular ears to see if he could hear out of it – and he could, just a little bit.

The only thing that Uncle Pinky ever wanted to be was a ball player. But three things kept him out of the game: One, he couldn't hit, Two, he couldn't catch, and Three, he was kind of an idiot. And then his hearing slowly went out. First the left ear, then the right ear… And eventually, all he had left was that tiny little third ear. Said it was like sucking the whole world through a straw.

Him and my dad once went to see Wrigley Field. Uncle Pinky had a friend there who was a custodian, and he let 'em out onto the field so they could see it from the right angle. And my dad walked up onto the pitcher's mound, and my Uncle Pinky picked up a bat, and they threw it around. And then, on the fifteenth pitch – wouldn't you know it – Uncle Pinky hit a moonshot that sailed out into the bleachers, just like Ernie Banks… You should'a seen it – pow… And he said he could hear the crowd roaring in his tiny little ear, even though no one was there.

He never swung at another ball again. 'cause that one shot, that one homer, was enough. And my darling, that is love – when you feel something in your heart for the longest time, and one moment fulfills it. And it rings in one little ear for a lifetime.

(fade)

Scene Five

*(**VERONICA**'s living room, a week later.)*

(A futon surrounded by still-packed boxes. Around are a few skeletons of animals, models of dinosaurs, molecules.)

*(**TRAVIS** and **VERONICA** edge through the front door, both of them carrying bags of groceries.)*

(They're in mid-conversation –)

VERONICA. – And I spent the rest of that summer taking apart owl poops and making little dioramas of mouse skeletons attacking each other. So welcome to my cottage.

TRAVIS. I like what you've done with the place. Jars of dead animals are supposed to be good feng shui.

VERONICA. You're dumb.

(She places a smaller grocery bag on the coffee table.)

TRAVIS. *(Re: his bag of groceries)* Where do you want this?

VERONICA. I got it.

(She takes the bags offstage into the kitchen.)

*(**TRAVIS** explores the room.)*

(He picks up a jar of paper cranes.)

TRAVIS. You have a jar of paper cranes.

(She re-enters.)

VERONICA. Yeah, when I quit smoking I folded them to keep my hands busy. It's fun.

TRAVIS. How many did you make?

VERONICA. Two thousand three hundred and sixteen. So, I promised that you were in for a treat –

(She hands him a package of tofu.)

TRAVIS. This is impossible. Where did you get this?

VERONICA. Shelby's grocery store.

TRAVIS. No, see, this is tofu. Shelby's grocery store doesn't carry tofu.

VERONICA. I know. I asked Frank to order it for me and he had it in a couple of days later.

TRAVIS. "Frank"? Chester's been trying to get "Frank" to carry tofu for years.

VERONICA. He should try asking nicely.

(heading into the kitchen)

Hey, you want some root beer? I brew it myself.

TRAVIS. Sure.

(She exits taking the tofu with her.)

*(***TRAVIS*** digs through the smaller grocery bag –)*

What else did you get Frank to carry?

VERONICA. *(off)* What?

(He comes up with a pair of Scratcher lottery tickets.)

TRAVIS. Scratcher tickets? You hoping for an early retirement?

(Hearing about the tickets, **VERONICA** *dashes back into the room –)*

VERONICA. No, I –

TRAVIS. Hold on, I've got a coin.

(He's about to scratch them off, but she stops him –)

VERONICA. Don't. Stop – please.

TRAVIS. Don't you want to see if you've won?

VERONICA. Give 'em to me.

TRAVIS. You don't trust me with your scratcher tickets?

VERONICA. No – I mean, yes, I trust you with my scratcher tickets. BUT –

TRAVIS. I've never won anything in my life, so statistically, I'm about due –

VERONICA. No, see, Travis… It's dumb, but… I collect them.

(She hands him a shoebox.)

(Inside are neatly organized stacks of scratcher tickets.)

VERONICA. *(cont.)* I've been collecting them for a while now.

*(**TRAVIS** looks through the tickets –)*

TRAVIS. "Lucky Dog"… "Cash Cow"… "High on the Hog"… And here you have the leprechaun section.

(She looks at the tickets fondly –)

VERONICA. Yeah.

TRAVIS. All very neatly organized and categorized –

VERONICA. Yeah. It's neat to see what images people associate with their dreams coming true. Animals, avalanches of gold coins, Genies…These are the last things people see before they find out if they're rich or disappointed.

TRAVIS. You don't want to scratch any of them off?

VERONICA. I don't need to be rich or disappointed.

(He takes out a single ticket.)

TRAVIS. "Rainbow's End."

VERONICA. Yes. My dad gave me that one when I was ten… I looked at it and thought, if I scratch this off, the moment vanishes. Each of these tickets is like a little moment of truth. It's fun to save them instead of spending them.

(beat)

And my dad owned a grocery, so I used to get paid in these for hauling gallons of milk.

TRAVIS. That's funny – most kids would've wanted an allowance.

VERONICA. I guess. Did you get an allowance?

TRAVIS. Yeah. In exchange for doing chores my parents would continue to feed me.

VERONICA. I heard from Maggie Reed that you're not from around these parts.

TRAVIS. Yeah. I moved down from L.A. a couple of years ago.

VERONICA. So what are you doing in Wyoming?

TRAVIS. Well, in L.A. I had this problem where I couldn't really sleep.

VERONICA. What do you mean?

TRAVIS. Every night I'd hear ambulances screaming in the distance. And I figured that eventually, one of them was going to come for me.

(beat)

Anyway, it doesn't matter where we teach these days. The kids all look the same, talk the same. Same gang signs.

VERONICA. It's good to have someone to talk to. My greatest fear was that I'd come out here and I'd be forced to adopt more cats.

TRAVIS. It takes a lot of guts to come out here by yourself –

VERONICA. Aren't you modest –

TRAVIS. I'm not...I'm just saying that it shows a great deal of courage on your part.

VERONICA. It's a pretty amazing thing though, you and me meeting here in the middle of nowhere.

TRAVIS. I was just thinking that.

(a short pause)

VERONICA. But I've decided that I'm going to use this year to clear my head. Live in a wide-open space and get good at being single.

TRAVIS. Oh, yeah... Well this is the place to do it.

VERONICA. Yeah, the Right Man keeps coming along and screwing up my life.

TRAVIS. The same guy?

VERONICA. Oh, no. Different guys. Right Men, I should say.

TRAVIS. I thought there was only supposed to be one Right Man.

VERONICA. Nah, they keep on coming. They show up like puppies on my rainy doorstep. And every time I think, "Hmm, he seems like the right one. Better let him in." Then a few months later there's an igloo of poo on my living room floor.

TRAVIS. Maybe you haven't met the right Right Man yet.

VERONICA. My boyfriends start out all neat and cool but eventually they de-evolve into Neanderthal ape men. Like Donald Dabbraccio. *(pron.* "dah-brac-ki-oh"*)*

TRAVIS. That sounds like a disease.

VERONICA. Yes, it does. And he was my first boyfriend. Donald Dabbraccio. The name says it all. There was something wrong with his saliva ducts. He had to put a sponge in his mouth before we could french kiss.

TRAVIS. *(laughing)* That's so sad.

VERONICA. Without the sponge it would be like making out with a bowl of soup.

TRAVIS. I had the same sort of situation with my first girlfriend. Hunter Kim. She was the only senior at our high school that still wore a retainer. But we made it romantic. She'd take it out at night and I'd clean it for her.

VERONICA. That's sweet.

TRAVIS. Nothing in the world smells worse than a kid's retainer. I only did it because I loved her.

VERONICA. So what happened?

TRAVIS. Eventually she began a career that consisted of being photographed while lying on the hoods of Japanese cars.

VERONICA. That's hot. But beat this: College. Ryan Perkins. Major stoner. He dealt to most of NYU. He could play a bong as a musical instrument.

TRAVIS. That's a highly sought-after skill.

VERONICA. Yeah. He could belt out any Grateful Dead song with bubbling noises. But eventually I found out that he was accepting sex for ounces.

TRAVIS. That sucks.

VERONICA. Yeah. The worst part was that he was still charging me.

TRAVIS. Well, my college girlfriend was this classic Korean bad girl. Karen Hong. She was on a full-ride scholarship from Crown Royal… Eventually we broke up and she became a born again virgin.

VERONICA. Wonderful. But that's nowhere as bad as my last boyfriend. Todd O'Reilly. I-Banker. Mr. Big-Time-Big-Shot-Big-Boy.

TRAVIS. What happened?

VERONICA. He grew a white powdery mustache… One of the reasons why I decided to get out of the city.

TRAVIS. Good reason.

VERONICA. So when was your last relationship?

TRAVIS. A while ago.

VERONICA. Tell me.

TRAVIS. It was before I left L.A. Her name was Grace.

VERONICA. Can't stay away from those Korean girls –

TRAVIS. She was the doctor of the family.

VERONICA. She was the doctor, the next kid was the lawyer –

TRAVIS. *(overlapping with "lawyer")* Her brother was the lawyer, her sister was the accountant. So she and I were pretty serious but her parents decided that… She should be with someone of equal standing. So one afternoon I walk up to my car and there's a letter on the windshield.

VERONICA. Just like that?

TRAVIS. Yeah. And when you find a breakup note on your car, it's time to get the hell out of L.A.

VERONICA. That's terrible. I'm sorry.

TRAVIS. It's okay. We move on, right?

VERONICA. Yup.

TRAVIS. *(recalls)* Donald Dabbraccio, Ryan Perkins, Todd O'Reilly. I see a pattern here.

VERONICA. Yes. You only go out with Asian women.

TRAVIS. I was going to say that you only go out with –

VERONICA. Don't start.

TRAVIS. Don't start what?

VERONICA. The lecture you're about to give me.

TRAVIS. I was just going to point out a particular taste in men that you have.

VERONICA. And what is that?

TRAVIS. Oh, I don't know –

VERONICA. I just get along better with, and I've always only been attracted to –

TRAVIS & VERONICA. *(together)* White guys –

VERONICA. Yes, and that's my business.

TRAVIS. Yeah, but why is that?

VERONICA. I don't know.

TRAVIS. You've never dated an Asian guy?

VERONICA. I have. Once.

TRAVIS. Well, I tried broccoli once, and I was sorta disappointed but I gave it a second chance.

VERONICA. Travis, does this bother you? You're acting as if this bothers you.

TRAVIS. Of course it bothers me. It's like when four out of five dentists recommend a brand of toothpaste. I'm like the crappy brand that the fifth guy recommends.

VERONICA. Look – it's what I'm used to and what I'm attracted to. And it's nobody's business –

TRAVIS. Fine.

VERONICA. So is that all right with you?

TRAVIS. Yeah.

VERONICA. Travis –

TRAVIS. No, it's fine with me.

VERONICA. Good. Because I don't want to find out that you're going to judge me just because of my likes and dislikes.

TRAVIS. All right. But for your information, I want you to know that I don't just date Asian women. I'm all over the color spectrum.

VERONICA. Oh yeah?

TRAVIS. Yeah. I once had this long, amazing relationship with this incredible Puerto Rican girl. A gymnast. Though I had to break it off with her when I found out that she had a fetish for Asian men.

VERONICA. Really?

TRAVIS. Yeah. She used to clip pictures out of Martial Artist Magazine.

VERONICA. Come on – we'd better get started on dinner. Let's see you work your magic.

TRAVIS. All right.

(as she exits –)

VERONICA. You make me feel good, Travis. I move out here to the middle of nowhere, and I still find someone to eat tofu with.

(He lags behind, staring at the scratcher tickets with a slight frown.)

Scene Six

(At center, **DEL** *addresses us directly:)*

(Letter #3:)

DEL. Bruce Lee, A.K.A. The Dragon, created the martial art form known as Jeet Kune Do by studying all of the martial arts and combining the best bits and pieces. I don't know if you've heard this story, but once, he discovered this Shaolin Master who could channel his energy, his CHI, into any part of his body and become invincible. So Bruce went to check out his technique. The master brought out his students to demonstrate. He said to one of them, "YOU – kick me in the stomach as hard as you can." And the master concentrated, channeled all of his Chi to his stomach – and the student KICKED him with all of his might… And nothing happened. The guy didn't even flinch. The master says to another student, "YOU – kick me in the face as hard as you can." Once again, the master concentrates all of his Chi, the student KICKS him in the face, and nothing. Not even a bruise. Bruce was impressed.

So the master says to Bruce, "All right, now you may punch me in the face as hard as you can." Bruce nods, the master concentrates all of his Chi, Bruce winds up… And KICKS HIM IN THE NUTS. And the master goes down clutching his crotch, gasping… And he says to Bruce, "Godammit, I told you to punch me in the face!"

And Bruce says, "I know, but at that particular moment, I really felt like kicking you in the nuts…Your technique is useless."

And that is love. It gets you when you least expect it. And no matter how much you prepare to take it on the chin, you never know when it's going to kick you in the nuts.

(fade)

Scene Seven

(Outdoors. Dusk.)

(Sound of crickets chirping, a light wind, the hum of a far away freeway.)

*(***DEL*** stands at the side, kneading his glove.)*

*(***TRAVIS*** is on the opposite side, also wearing a baseball glove.)*

*(***TRAVIS*** pitches an invisible ball at ***DEL***, who catches it.)*

DEL. *(reciting from memory and often messing up)* Ladies and gentlemen, welcome to Cheyenne Pete's Wild West Show and Indoor Rodeo –

TRAVIS. *(coaching him through)* Yee-haw. Don't forget the yee-haw, it's important –

(They pitch the ball back and forth, playing catch –)

DEL. Right. Yee-haw. I am Cheyenne Pete, your head honcho for this evening's...

TRAVIS. Entertainment –

DEL. Entertainment; you are about to witness the most earth-shaking –

TRAVIS. Earthshaking-est –

DEL. Earthshaking-est, most breathtaking buffalo –

TRAVIS. Breathtaking-est –

DEL. Goddamn – Breathtaking-est buffalo and bronco blowout...Uh...

TRAVIS. *(finishing it)* This side of the Mississippi. We got Figure-Eight trick ropers, we got Ornery Owen the Horn-Ed steer – but don't you worry 'cause the arena you see before you is TRIPLE RE-INFORCED – and if you'd like an autograph from a real live Indian, please ask your server. Now, get ready to cheer for your section's cowboy, 'cause Cheyenne Pete's Wild West Show has just begun. Yee-haw.

(beat)

You were supposed to have that memorized.

DEL. Hold on.

(He produces a half-smoked joint, lights it, takes a long drag –)

Okay. From the top.

TRAVIS. Is that a joint?

DEL. It helps me remember things. Gets me relaxed. I get a little stoned, go over what I need to know, and when it comes time to repeat the information, I get stoned again and it comes right back to me.

TRAVIS. So you were stoned when you were memorizing your lines?

DEL. No. But I am now relaxed.

TRAVIS. You shouldn't be smoking weed, Del. You're a teacher for christ's sake.

DEL. I'm a P.E. teacher. And this isn't even my weed. It's Bill's weed. So if I ever get caught smoking it, I'll just say, "Dad, Sir, this is not my weed. It's Bill's. I found it in his room – see, he buys it from a quarter-Indian dealer named Mystery Dream. So as you can see, Sir, Bill is just as much of a hucklefuck as your other son. Me."

TRAVIS. That's good, that'll show him. You want to work on your audition now?

DEL. I don't wanna audition for Cheyenne Pete's anymore, Travis. That speech was probably written by a Texan.

TRAVIS. You can't move off of your dad's ranch on a part-time P.E. teacher's salary.

DEL. I know.

TRAVIS. So what are you going to do?

DEL. Man, I dunno.

(He pinches out the joint and sticks it in his mouth.)

(He puts his glove back on.)

Toss me the ball.

(The game of catch resumes.)

You met the new teacher?

TRAVIS. Veronica? Yeah.

DEL. She's from New York City, Travis. New York City.

TRAVIS. You've talked to her?

DEL. Aww…naw, man. I wouldn't know what to say. She's different.

TRAVIS. What do you mean, different?

DEL. She's not like the girls around here, not like the girls on TV… She's Ko-rean, right? Hooo – I didn't expect a Ko-rean girl to look like that.

TRAVIS. What did you think they looked like?

DEL. I dunno. Like you in a wig?

*(***TRAVIS** *pitches a fastball that slams, hard, into* **DEL***'s mitt.* **DEL** *notices the extra heat on it –)*

Ow…what?

TRAVIS. It's funny how a beautiful woman transcends all racial boundaries.

DEL. What's that?

TRAVIS. A beautiful Asian woman moves into town and you're biting your fist at how fine she is. But when I moved in? "Hey Jap! Go back to China!"

DEL. So you're still holding that over my head.

TRAVIS. I just think it's funny, that's all.

DEL. I didn't know you back then. I thought you were a tourist. I didn't even know you could speak English.

TRAVIS. I'm touched.

DEL. Yeap, I'm in-the-know now. I'm sensitive to things.

*(***DEL** *begins to quietly chant her name as he winds up and pitches –)*

Verrr-onica… Lee-lee-lee-lee…

TRAVIS. You really like her.

DEL. Why'dya say that?

TRAVIS. You're doing that lee-lee-lee-lee thing.

DEL. She's pretty.

TRAVIS. Why don't you introduce yourself?

DEL. I sorta already tried.

TRAVIS. And?

DEL. I saw her in your classroom at the beginning of lunch. And I dunno, I just kind of stood in the doorway for a little while trying to think of something to say. But she just looked so damn professional, y'know? And before I could speak up, she said, "Hey – you gotta mop up a bit more around the door 'cause one of the kids threw up during first period. And also please empty the trash on your way out 'cause you forgot to do it last night. Thanks." And when I got back from emptying out the trash, she was gone. Which is good, I guess, 'cause on the way to the dumpster I was rackin' my brain for something to say and I couldn't think of nothin'.

TRAVIS. What's the problem? You don't have any trouble talking to other women.

DEL. I know the girls around here. We got a common thing going. But not Veronica. She's got that big city get-the-hell-outta-my-way thing going on… And she's Ko-rean.

TRAVIS. So what if she's Ko-rean? She's just like everybody else. The only difference between us and her is that she's fine as hell.

DEL. I know. It messes up my train of thought.

(beat)

So I was gonna ask you if maybe you could help me out.

TRAVIS. What am I supposed to do?

DEL. You lived in a big city. And, you're Ko-rean, too – you don't know what it's like living here all your life. You've been other places, seen things.

TRAVIS. So what?

DEL. My whole life it's been the same stuff. The same people. And I want something different.

TRAVIS. Why don't you write her a note or something?

DEL. Yeah! What?

TRAVIS. A note: a non-verbal communication written on a piece of paper –

DEL. I know what a note is, Travis. I've written 'em many times to myself.

TRAVIS. So go. Activate.

DEL. But what's it supposed to say?

TRAVIS. Everything you just said to me right now sounds pretty good.

DEL. No it doesn't. It don't sound good, Travis. You gotta make it sound good, see? And you – you're good with words – I always see you readin' some book or other –

TRAVIS. Sure.

DEL. You're good at communicating with people, Travis. You're an English teacher – your job is to put words together –

TRAVIS. No. My job is to give kids books so they can draw penises in the margins.

DEL. All I need is a little cheat-sheet or something. Write something for me.

TRAVIS. Get off me.

DEL. Come on Travis. Please.

TRAVIS. I don't even know if it'll do any good. She says that she's intent on being single.

DEL. But why not give it a shot? "Stories are powerful" – that's what you say. So maybe write me a little story.

(A pause as **TRAVIS** *considers this.)*

TRAVIS. All right.

DEL. *(elated)* Thanks Travis. I owe you, man.

TRAVIS. No more weed. That's my asking price.

DEL. Done.

(He makes a grand ceremonial gesture of tossing the joint away.)

DEL. By the way, I'm sorry I called you a Jap before.

TRAVIS. It's okay. I get it all the time.

(They continue to play catch.)

Scene Eight

(The classroom, the next day.)

(Some of the animal skeletons and dinosaur models from **VERONICA***'s living room are now present.)*

*(***TRAVIS** *sits in one of the student chairs writing on a piece of paper with a great deal of concentration.)*

*(***CHESTER** *stands behind the teacher's desk. He bangs a gavel.)*

CHESTER. Order! I call this BAAA Meeting to order. Will the Secretary please read the last week's minutes?

TRAVIS. *(without looking up)* Screw you.

CHESTER. Fine. But please note that if the Secretary continues to behave in a surly manner, he may find himself in Poor Standing with this organization. Furthermore, a member in Poor Standing may be removed from the –

(Lights fade on **CHESTER** *as his voice drowns out.)*

*(***TRAVIS** *reads what he has just written back to himself:)*

TRAVIS. Dear Veronica, Things in nature always hide... Lizards change the color of their skins... Moths live or die based on the color of their wings... To stand out in the world is to invite danger. You will be swallowed alive by something that was waiting for you to show yourself.
But now I throw away my fear –

(He writes something in, then...)

Signed...

*(***TRAVIS** *signs the letter.)*

(Suddenly, lights up on **CHESTER** *–)*

CHESTER. Travis, are you listening to me?

TRAVIS. Yeah. I've been kicked out of your gang.

CHESTER. That was five minutes ago. Now we're onto the railroad thing.

TRAVIS. What railroad thing?

CHESTER. Hello?! The Central Pacific Railroad Celebration? The mayor has been planning it for weeks. A jolly top-hatted crew of Deathmongers are riding a train along the original route of the railroad. And of course, their literature totally omits the thankless roles suffered by our people: China men dynamited off mountains, their bones picked clean at the bottom of forgotten valleys. So when they stop in town to hoo-hah and pat themselves on their fat little backs, we'll be waiting for them.

(He holds up various hastily-crafted picket signs that say things like "RIDE BACK OUT ON YOUR RAIL," "INDENTURE THIS," and "FUCK YOU.")

TRAVIS. All right, Chester. I'm with you.

CHESTER. *(surprised and elated)* You are? Finally!

TRAVIS. I'll talk to the organizers and see if our school can put something together about the Chinese railroad workers.

CHESTER. Yellow Power in Action, Yellow People in Action!

TRAVIS. But personally, I think the picket signs are a bad idea.

(beat)

On second thought, give me that one.

(He points at the sign that says "FUCK YOU.")

*(**CHESTER** gives him the sign.)*

TRAVIS. This might come in handy sometime.

CHESTER. The railroad celebration will be in a few weeks. So you might want to jot that down in your notes –

*(He snatches the letter from **TRAVIS**'s hands.)*

TRAVIS. Hey!

CHESTER. *(reads)* Things in nature…roaring, dancing… I am a frog. I am birds… So here I am. Signed… DEL?

(furious)

What are you doing, man?

TRAVIS. I'm helping out a friend.

CHESTER. You mean you're helping The Man to OUR woman –

TRAVIS. Our…? Our woman? As in "Including You"-OUR woman?

CHESTER. You're like a Chinese waiter giving him a fork! You know what, Travis? I never wanted to say this to your face, but I've got to now: You're a Twinkie.

TRAVIS. I am not a Twinkie.

CHESTER. *(shakes the note)* Then what's this? Not only are you in love with The Man, you're writing love letters on his behalf. Hasn't the Asian Man suffered enough?

TRAVIS. It doesn't matter. I don't have a shot with her.

CHESTER. My Brother, you gotta lift that fist and raise up that self-esteem.

TRAVIS. No, see, Veronica… She only goes out with –

CHESTER. Goes out with what?

TRAVIS. White men.

(A pause as this sinks in.)

CHESTER. Ooooooo. Ooooooo… I'm gonna… I'm gonna go over to her house and… Gimme back my sign!

TRAVIS. Relax, Chester.

CHESTER. I knew she was the type that tongued for snowflakes! Playing a piano with no sharps or flats, is she? I guess that's the way it goes for the Asian Man, isn't it? Not only is she not-down with us, but she's trying to jump from the field into the motherfuckin' house!

TRAVIS. Veronica has a right to have her own preferences.

CHESTER. I thought I had to make up the balance for only one Twinkie in this town – but now I gotta deal with a whole snack-pack of you traitors. And you're helping Del? DEL?! A man whose social and cultural center is the parking lot at Safeway? Whose Brother are you supposed to be?

TRAVIS. I'm nobody's brother. I'm just a guy helping out a friend. If she's not going to go for me, I might as well help him out. I'm not –

CHESTER. Asian –

TRAVIS. I wasn't gonna say Asian –

CHESTER. But you want to.

TRAVIS. Yes. I mean – no. Look, don't try to politicize this.

CHESTER. EVERYTHING is political. Don't you see that? You and I are the Fortress of Asian America in this town – and it will die without us. If you were a true Korean Brother, you'd see that. *Han gook mal arra?*

(**TRAVIS** *pauses, bewildered –)*

TRAVIS. Oh God, no.

CHESTER. I don't know why I couldn't put my finger on it earlier.

(points to his face)

Just look at these cheekbones.

TRAVIS. Don't you dare –

CHESTER. And now that I've embraced my Korean heritage, I'm seeing you in a whole new light.

TRAVIS. If you do turn out to be Korean, I'm definitely switching to something else.

*(***CHESTER** *crumples up the note and tosses it at* **TRAVIS***.)*

CHESTER. Do whatever you want. Write your little letters for Whitey McWhiteman. See what I care. I know I've always been on my own, a Ronin, masterless. And BAAA has always been an army of one. I just never wanted to believe it.

TRAVIS. When are you going to see that it's not about white, black, Asian, or whatever? We are all just people, Chester. Confused people, and it doesn't matter what the color of the wrapping paper is.

CHESTER. Tell that to your purely-platonic friend with the preferences.

*(***CHESTER** *exits.)*

*(***TRAVIS** *picks up the crumpled piece of paper, straightens it, and puts it into his pocket.)*

Scene Nine

(The classroom, a couple of weeks later.)

*(***TRAVIS*** sits at the desk typing as* **DEL** *watches over his shoulder.)*

TRAVIS. *(as he continues to type throughout –)* Almost done.

DEL. Thanks for writing these for me, Travis. She can't stop talking about them.

TRAVIS. So they've been working for you?

DEL. Yeah. Ever since I put the first one in her mailbox. The next day she comes right up to me, invites me over for dinner. And I seen her every night this week.

TRAVIS. Every night, huh?

DEL. Yeap. All thanks to you.

TRAVIS. So what have you two been doing together?

DEL. Oh, man, Travis – everything. Watch movies, eat cheeseburgers, play basketball, take pictures. We dance... Did you know she has a trampoline, Travis?

TRAVIS. No.

DEL. She has a trampoline, Travis! And we read your letters together.

(beat)

Goddamn, they bring me back. Your stories, my stories, all mixed up together. I didn't know you and me combined could be so interesting.

TRAVIS. Me either.

DEL. Don't think that I don't appreciate this. You're going above and beyond the call of what you gotta do – you're giving me more than I even need. And I thank you for that.

*(***TRAVIS*** hits a last key with a satisfying click, and whips the page out of the typewriter.)*

What's this one about?

TRAVIS. My uncle. He had three ears.

DEL. Thanks.

(**DEL** *signs the letter and pockets it.*)

So I got a question for you.

TRAVIS. Yeah?

DEL. Why don't you ever try to get anyone yourself?

TRAVIS. What are you talking about?

DEL. You've been single ever since I've known you. Why's that?

TRAVIS. There's no one in this town that I'm attracted to.

DEL. No one.

TRAVIS. Nope.

DEL. Come on... Daisy Sherwood – not attractive?

TRAVIS. No. Her head's too small. She wears those big hoop earrings to make her head look normal-sized, but it doesn't work.

DEL. Clarissa Jones?

TRAVIS. No. She's got that fe-mullet going on. Very unattractive.

DEL. Harriet Mackenzie?

TRAVIS. No. She looks too much like her sister.

DEL. Janie Mackenzie?

TRAVIS. No. She looks too much like her sister.

DEL. Big Roy? Little Roy? Heck?

TRAVIS. Now, Heck is very handsome for an eighty year-old man, but he's got crazy-eyes from that long-ago bout with Syphilis.

DEL. I don't get you, Travis. You live your life in right field, and it ain't right. A man can't go forever without affection. We're supposed to cuddle.

TRAVIS. I moved here because I wanted to live in a small town. Get away from complications.

DEL. Complications are good. Before I met Veronica the only complex thing in my life was numbering the school's basketballs. But complications, attractions n' shit – these are good things! I mean, not to sound fruity or nothin', 'cause you know I'm All Man.

TRAVIS. Right.

DEL. And look at you – you're very handsome for a Ko-rean fella.

TRAVIS. Thanks. Most of us have large humps on our backs and monobrows.

DEL. You know what I mean. You're a good guy, and you have a good old soul. And with charm like this you could get any girl in this town…
But you're still hiding from her.

TRAVIS. From who?

DEL. Come on. Never mind all the hoo-hah about small towns and complications. You're still hiding from Grace.

TRAVIS. Grace was a long time ago.

DEL. I know. So –

*(**TRAVIS** turns away, inserts a new page into the type-writer.)*

I'm just lookin' out, Travis. After all, winter's coming. It's a bad time to find yourself alone.

*(**DEL** exits.)*

*(**TRAVIS** stares at the blank page.)*

(And he begins to type.)

Scene Ten

(At center, **DEL** *addresses us directly:)*

(Letter #4:)

DEL. Just like you, my dad loved movies. Specifically, spaghetti westerns. "American Made in Italy," he'd call them. But he would never go see a movie alone. "What kind of loser sees a movie by himself?" he'd say. He'd rather sit at home on a Friday night than bear the public humiliation of going to a movie theater by himself.

But when he met my mom, everything changed. From then on, he loved seeing movies by himself.

He'd get the extra-large tub of popcorn and put his feet up on the seat, make a grand show of being there by himself. He said it was because he knew that he had someone in his life – that he truly wasn't alone. People could think whatever they wanted, but they would be wrong.

He felt like a king sitting up there, sneaking in beers. And when the lights came up at the end, he'd always find his way back to her.

And when things got bad at home, that's where he'd be. At the Royale watching *The Good, The Bad, and The Ugly,* just him and Clint Eastwood.

And when she finally left him, that was still where he went.

(short pause)

What a fragile thing it is.

When you have it you might not know it, and when it's gone, it's as if it never mattered.

Because what the old man never realized was that he was always alone.

He was alone the entire time, with or without her.

(fade)

Scene Eleven

(The classroom, a few days later.)

*(***VERONICA*** sits in a student chair reading a letter.)*

*(***TRAVIS*** is at the teacher's desk, grading papers.)*

TRAVIS. What does that one say?

VERONICA. It's about spiders. Spiders that his cousin put on a twig to make them fight.

(She holds up another letter –)

This one's about atomic cold fusion.

(reads)

"We are fusion reactors reacting to each other, feeding off of this energy that comes out of nowhere – "

(beat)

It's dumb.

TRAVIS. Spiders and reactors, huh?

VERONICA. Spiders, reactors, baseball, Bruce Lee. Bruce Lee! I detect the influence of your friendship.

TRAVIS. Hmm.

VERONICA. Sometimes they're silly, sometimes they're serious…and they all fit together like a conversation. It's amazing. When I first saw him I noticed that sweet little cowboy smile of his. But I never saw…I never guessed that these kind of thoughts could be behind it.

TRAVIS. I guess some things are easier to say on paper.

VERONICA. I'm falling, Travis. I've fallen.

TRAVIS. What happened to getting good at being single?

VERONICA. That policy has been dismantled. It lies dead and buried next to my anger at the male species.

TRAVIS. It's nice to see you smiling like that.

VERONICA. Yeah. Because he's also a gorgeous specimen of manhood.

TRAVIS. So it's moving pretty quickly between the two of you?

VERONICA. Yeah. I've even tried looking for speed bumps and road kill, but I just can't find any. And I'm positive that he's not one of those slimy guys with an Asian Fetish.

TRAVIS. How's that?

VERONICA. I located his porn stash.

(She produces a small, heavy cardboard box. It lands on the desk with a thump.)

TRAVIS. And you brought it to school to show me?

VERONICA. Travis, if this is the first time you've ever seen pornography and you feel uncomfortable, it's okay to let me know.

(She starts going through it.)

The truth in a man's heart can be found in his porn stash. I found it in the default hiding spot – the sock drawer.

TRAVIS. Brilliant.

VERONICA. I am the master of locating porn stashes.

(She shows the contents to **TRAVIS** *[videotapes, magazines] –)*

It's your standard red-blooded American pornographic bric-a-brac. "Up-And-Cummers #23." "Dirty Debutantes"... No "East Meats West" with "meats" spelled M-E-A-T-S. No "Eastern Anal Odysseys." Nothing titled "Oriental Rug-Munchers" or "Dragon FIST-ing." Do you know what this means?

TRAVIS. I think so.

VERONICA. He's into me for me.

TRAVIS. Is that supposed to be surprising?

VERONICA. It's surprising when there are so few obstacles. The only ones are his dad and his asshole-brother Bill. He makes chinky-eyes at me.

TRAVIS. Ah, don't worry about Bill. He's just bitter because he failed to break into the sport of Monster Trucking.

(She puts the box away.)

VERONICA. So. After next semester I think I'm going to stay.

TRAVIS. Hey – that's great.

VERONICA. Yeah. I called my dad and I told him that I'm staying. But I don't think he understands why.

TRAVIS. He probably misses you.

VERONICA. No. He can't understand why I don't just stay back east and have kids already and be done with it. And I don't know how to explain that…you know. His English isn't so good and my Korean is pretty much crap.

TRAVIS. Yeah. My parents never really got fluent in English. For instance, they're Catholic, right, and you know the concept of transubstantiation? Where the bread turns into Jesus's flesh?

VERONICA. Yeah.

TRAVIS. My dad explained it to me like this: He said: "It looks like bread, it tastes like bread, but it's not bread anymore. It's Jesus."

VERONICA. That's hilarious.

(beat)

Well, I wish my dad would make an attempt to improve his English. Even after years of dealing with the customers in his store, he can't even understand when they're mocking him.

TRAVIS. Or maybe he doesn't care.

VERONICA. He could at least learn to speak better English for his kids.

TRAVIS. But he's old and he's probably set in his ways, and I think that's okay.

VERONICA. He stays cooped up in his little apartment and watches TV all night. And my sister's in Seattle and my brother doesn't give a shit, so it was up to me to check in on him. And now they're mad because I won't be able to do that anymore. But he barely says anything to me anyway.

(beat)

Listen, I'm sorry to lay this out on you.

TRAVIS. It's fine.

VERONICA. Of all the new people in my life, you're the only one that can understand.

(She picks up the box –)

I'd better put this porn stash back in its sock drawer.

TRAVIS. Oh, hey – I discovered a certain Chinese restaurant in Chugwater. They go through this distributor that can do small orders, and... This Friday, for the first time since I left California, I will have in my possession a jar of kimchee. So I was thinking that night we could get together and –

VERONICA. I'd like that.

TRAVIS. Yeah?

VERONICA. But maybe next week. Del and I are going up to the mountains this weekend.

TRAVIS. Oh. Well, it'll still be around when you get back.

VERONICA. But you don't have to wait around for me. You should enjoy it yourself.

TRAVIS. I'll bring you an extra jar. My treat.

VERONICA. Thanks. I'll see you tomorrow.

TRAVIS. See you tomorrow.

(She exits. Fade.)

Scene Twelve

(Later. The classroom.)

*(***TRAVIS*** sits at a student desk reading over a letter.)*

*(***DEL*** peeks his head in, knocks on the door.)*

DEL. I was sitting at the counter eatin' a piece of pie at Scullard's and a certain mutual friend of ours was parked right there next to me. Guess who it was.

*(***DEL*** enters.)*

TRAVIS. Daisy –

DEL. *(overlapping)* Daisy Sherwood. And we got to talking about traveling, and she asked if I'd ever been out of the country before and I said "No, but you know who has?"

TRAVIS. Travis –

DEL. Mr. Travis Park has. He's been all over the goddamned place. Well, I didn't say goddamn 'cause she bowls at the church, but you know what I mean.

TRAVIS. Thanks Del, but Daisy Sherwood and I have nothing in common.

DEL. Yes, you do! You both love to…uh…you're both ambitious. She's doing that art school through the internet and you've already got a degree and everything. And you both play sports. You both bowl –

TRAVIS. If I make a move on Daisy, I'll let you know. Here.

*(***TRAVIS*** hands the letter to ***DEL****.)*

DEL. What's this one about?

TRAVIS. It's about how you spent years trying to teach your dog how to drink through a straw.

DEL. Oh yeah. Thanks, Travis.

So if you say you don't have anything in common with Daisy Sherwood, who do you have something in common with?

TRAVIS. Why do you keep pestering me about this? I'm genuinely touched by your concern, but I'm doing all right. I got my deck built around my house, I've almost finished my barbecue made out of beer bottles and my soap carved chess set and I am *this* close to bowling a perfect game –

DEL. You come here at six in the morning, you teach these kids, you have dinner on Mondays, Wednesdays, and Fridays at Scullard's by yourself, and every other day you eat at home, alone.

TRAVIS. Yeah –

DEL. You read alone at the library, you drive an hour and a half just to rent videos to watch alone. And that ain't right, Travis. That's somebody else's life.

TRAVIS. Maybe I like living this way. Maybe it beats the hell out of L.A. traffic and smog and –

DEL. But lemme ask you somethin' – don't you want anything more?

(short pause)

'cause I read your letters.

TRAVIS. Where's this coming from?

DEL. Last night I decided that…I have to tell you that I don't think you should write the letters to her anymore.

TRAVIS. Why?

DEL. 'cause I'm moving in with her. And she doesn't need them anymore.

(beat)

It'll be good to not have to wake up to oily pancakes with my dad and the guests. It'll be good to have a place to be. To be with her.

(a short pause)

She asks me questions that I can't answer. There are details I can't fill in. And you were right to begin with – I should be tellin' her things about my life. So you don't have to write the letters anymore, okay Travis? 'cause I don't think it's right. For you either.

TRAVIS. What do you mean, "for me either"?

DEL. Nothin'.

TRAVIS. 'cause all this is for you, Del.

DEL. No. You…you need to stop writing them. Okay, Travis?

TRAVIS. Is she happy, Del?

DEL. Yeah. She is.

(beat)

I want you to pay Daisy Sherwood some mind, all right? And let's throw the ball around sometime, okay? It's been a while.

*(**DEL** exits.)*

*(**TRAVIS** takes a deep breath, surveys the room. He sits at the teacher's desk, aimless.)*

Scene Thirteen

(At center, **DEL** *addresses us directly:)*

(Letter #5:)

DEL. My grandfather kept over two hundred horses. There was a sea of them, rolling over our land. You would have loved to see that sight. Me, I can barely remember it. See, over time their numbers were decimated as we went from keeping horses to keeping tourists from New Jersey.

As a boy, it was my job to feed and water the horses we had left. And like a person, every horse is a mix of clever and crazy, courageous, calm and cunning.

I had a horse named Blue – blue because his gray coat had a tinge of it – and in the mix of that horse there was more crazy than anything else.

I loved that horse. He took to no one else but me. He was the first thing that was ever mine.

And he was mine until I was seventeen. There was the night when I woke up and saw an orange glint on my window. I looked out and saw the glow from across the circle – the stables were burning. They were disintegrating, being eaten alive by smoke.

I tried to wake my brother but he wouldn't budge. I pushed my dad out of bed, and we all rushed out with buckets, blew open the doors to let out the horses. And they came streaming out, panicked. And then I saw him.

He dragged himself out into the air like a crippled old man. His flesh was charred black, and there were tears in his skin through which you could see red. He was silent.

And there I was. And I didn't know how to save him.

And that is love, I think. Because maybe love isn't, by itself, a feeling. But the absence of love – of losing it – is. It eats us alive. It murders us.

(fade)

End of Act One

ACT TWO

Scene One

(The classroom, a few weeks later.)

(There's a muffled groan from behind the door.)

(A few more, getting louder, then **TRAVIS** *enters dragging in* **CHESTER**, *who staggers in drunk.)*

CHESTER. Victory! Victory! Yellow people, yellow power! Yellow power, yellow people!

*(***CHESTER** *carries several papîer mache severed limbs and a busted protest sign [from earlier]. He is covered in what appears to be blood.)*

(He groans as **TRAVIS** *helps him into a student desk chair.)*

I got the bastards.

*(***TRAVIS** *takes a roll of paper towels out his desk and cleans* **CHESTER***'s face up.)*

TRAVIS. Sit still.

CHESTER. Did you hear that fat Animal Farm pig of an engineer yell, "Get that chink bastard off the tracks?" Little did Ignorant know that I'm Japanese.

TRAVIS. How much did you drink?

CHESTER. Not much. Jack Daniels. Just a little. Quart.

TRAVIS. You've really outdone yourself this time.

CHESTER. I was only exercising my right to free assembly and speech.

TRAVIS. Little Roy bursts into my kitchen yelling for me to get down to the tracks. When I get there everybody's in mob formation, and there you are, lying in front of the celebration train, covered in fake blood and surrounded by body parts –

CHESTER. *(re: the severed limbs)* These represent the pieces of our fallen ancestors.

TRAVIS. Why do you insist on making a fool out of yourself?

CHESTER. Are you afraid that my behavior casts a yellow stain on your lily-white reputation?

TRAVIS. Yes, I am. Because half the people in town can't tell us apart.

CHESTER. Some of us refuse to cooperate with the establishment. We are non-cooperational, and we have to take matters into our own hands. Because we aren't going to take things lying down. Even though, we sometimes have to lie down in order to stand up for ourselves.

TRAVIS. You know Hallsey's looking for you, right? If we hadn't gotten out of there, you'd be in a cell right now.

CHESTER. Let him come. There's no way he's gonna get me.

TRAVIS. And how's that?

CHESTER. 'cause I'm a fucking Samurai, is why.

(beat)

And even though I'm lost in the wilderness of America, I don't care. And I don't care that I don't have a Brother anymore.

(He tries to get up but **TRAVIS** *eases him back into his seat.)*

TRAVIS. You're going to stay here until you've sobered up and quieted down. Then I'm taking you home.

CHESTER. I'm not going back to Randall and Betty's basement. There are fifteen taxidermied deer heads that stare at me while I sleep. And it stinks.

TRAVIS. Quiet down or I'll take you home right now.

*(***CHESTER** *leaps to his feet –)*

CHESTER. I'M NOT GOING BACK!

(Something heavy and wrapped in black cloth falls out of **CHESTER***'s pocket and hits the ground with a thud.)*

*(***CHESTER** *makes a swipe for it, but* **TRAVIS** *beats him to it.)*

*(**TRAVIS** unwraps the object: A five-and-a-half inch golden railroad spike.)*

CHESTER. You were not supposed to see that.

TRAVIS. What is this?

CHESTER. It's the Last Spike.

TRAVIS. The real –

CHESTER. The real Last Spike. Hammered into the ground in 1869 by Leland Stanford at Promontory, Utah. To celebrate the joining of the two halves of this chunky country.

TRAVIS. It's heavy.

CHESTER. Seventy-five percent of it is gold.

TRAVIS. My God.

CHESTER. Look at it, so shiny and innocent-seeming. And yet, this object is the pinnacle of a mountain of blown-up Chinamen. Its home was once a velvet cushion in the halls of Stanford University. But then the Railroad Tour brought it here.

(beat)

Look at it, Travis. It's caused us so much pain. But now it's come home to its rightful owner: The Asian Man.

(A pause as this sinks in.)

TRAVIS. You're not keeping it.

CHESTER. You're right. I'm not.

(recites)

"Dear Stanford University, we have your artifact of atrocious history. If you want it back, prepare a hundred thousand dollars in unmarked bills. P.S. – fuck you."

TRAVIS. You can't hold this thing for ransom!

CHESTER. I'm going to do good with the money, Travis. I'm going to water the seeds of Asian America from east to west. I'm gonna bring the gospel of Bruce. That spike is my ticket out of this goddamned town. It's my escape pod.

TRAVIS. You're nuts.

CHESTER. I am sick of having to avert my eyes when they call me by their list of slurs. I wanna be set off like a firecracker. I wanna see an ocean.

(beat)

Do you see, Travis? That spike was our past, beaten into the ground in the middle of nowhere. It kept us hammered down. But now it will set us free. That spike is me.

TRAVIS. No, it's not. It's going back.

*(***TRAVIS*** wraps up the spike.)*

CHESTER. No –

TRAVIS. I'm going to keep it safe until the heat's off. Hallsey can turn your parents' place upside down and he won't be able to find it –

CHESTER. No –

TRAVIS. And then I'm going to send it back to Stanford with a note that says that it was all a stupid prank –

CHESTER. NO!

*(***CHESTER*** makes a grab for the spike but* **TRAVIS** *edges out of the way.)*

TRAVIS. You're not going to get it.

CHESTER. I will use force, Travis.

TRAVIS. Let's see you try.

CHESTER. Is this what your Twinkification has brought you to? Asian-on-Asian violence?

*(***CHESTER*** pulls a pair of nunchucks out of his pocket.)*

Maybe I shouldn't mind so much. After all, you are standing in the path of The Revolution.

(They circle each other slowly, **CHESTER** *swinging the nunchucks,* **TRAVIS** *feinting and dodging.)*

(Suddenly, **CHESTER** *screams, whirls the nunchucks around and whacks* **TRAVIS** *in the arm –)*

TRAVIS. OW! You hit me in the arm!

CHESTER. Oh, sorry, I –

*(**TRAVIS** whips around and puts **CHESTER** in a full nelson.)*

*(**CHESTER** struggles and drops the nunchucks.)*

*(They twist and buckle as **TRAVIS**' grip tightens –)*

TRAVIS. I will not let you burn yourself down. Not for some stupid –

CHESTER. It's not stupid!

TRAVIS. You call yourself Asian, but you don't know a thing about it. You read magazines and books, you wear costumes and you call that your identity –

CHESTER. IT'S ALL I'VE GOT.

*(**TRAVIS** slowly lets him go.)*

*(**CHESTER** is sobbing and blubbering now –)*

TRAVIS. Chester…please…get up.

CHESTER. I wanna show her who I am, Travis.

TRAVIS. Who are you talking about?

CHESTER. I love her. I love Veronica Lee.

TRAVIS. No, you don't.

CHESTER. Yes, I do. I wanna curl up against the nape of her neck, let her hair drape over my eyes and hide them forever.

TRAVIS. You've just never seen an Asian woman before.

CHESTER. Don't protect me. I am not harmless. I am harmful – I am full of harm. So let me go. I wanna find my own Veronica Lee.

TRAVIS. C'mon. On your feet.

*(**TRAVIS** helps **CHESTER** to his feet.)*

CHESTER. Why don't you let her see the truth? Why do you lie to her? At least you know who you are.

TRAVIS. I'm just a person.

CHESTER. You hide yourself. Even though you have everything to show.

TRAVIS. Go home. Go home and go to sleep, and don't make eye-contact with anyone on the way there. Lay low until I can figure out what to do.

*(**CHESTER** nods and slogs toward the door.)*

(He turns around –)

CHESTER. Can I have my spike back?

TRAVIS. No. Go home.

CHESTER. She gives her love to the wrong man. You throw it away.

(He exits.)

*(**TRAVIS** locks the spike up in his desk.)*

(He paces around, blowing off steam.)

(He gathers the pieces of garbage on the stage. He picks up the nunchucks.)

(He puts them in his pocket.)

Scene Two

(Late. **VERONICA***'s living room.)*

(There's a knock at the front door.)

*(***VERONICA** *answers it.)*

(It's **TRAVIS***.)*

TRAVIS. I ran out of my house as soon as I got your message. What happened?

VERONICA. Bad stuff, Travis.

TRAVIS. What's going on?

VERONICA. I left my garage door open and the fence was open and one of Dr. Peters' horses wandered into my garage and I came out and she was licking a puddle of antifreeze –

TRAVIS. My God.

VERONICA. So I called Dr. Peters and he called the vet and they took her away and now she's gonna die.

TRAVIS. No, she's not. They'll pump her stomach or something –

VERONICA. No. The antifreeze is going to destroy her kidneys and she's going to die.

TRAVIS. Her kidneys are going to be fine –

VERONICA. And Dr. Peters is being so goddamned nice but I just want him to get mad at me, y'know?

TRAVIS. The horse is going to be fine –

VERONICA. I want him to tell me that I that I'm a horse killer, that I fucked up –

TRAVIS. Okay, listen: When I was three years old I drank antifreeze.

VERONICA. What?

TRAVIS. I drank antifreeze when I was three years old. We were visiting my uncle in Canada. I found this bottle of antifreeze with the lid off and drank it. I remember that it tasted like punch.

VERONICA. You're lying.

TRAVIS. My mom found me, she freaked out, they took me to the hospital. Pumped my stomach. Then on the way home, in a fit of rage, my dad threw my uncle out of a moving car.

VERONICA. Get out –

TRAVIS. They didn't speak to each other for two years. And my kidneys are okay, and I'm fine. So Dr. Peters' horse is gonna be all right. You aren't a horse killer, okay?

VERONICA. Yes, I am.

TRAVIS. No, you're not. Animals are tough. When I was a kid I had a dog that used to eat glass.

VERONICA. Shut up.

TRAVIS. His name was Reggie. Eating glass was like his hobby or something. They had to operate on him twice to take things out of him. And one day, he broke into this packet of razor blades –

VERONICA. Okay, you're just messing with me now.

TRAVIS. Yes, I am.

VERONICA. So stop.

TRAVIS. Okay.

(a short pause)

VERONICA. I watch them from my window. The horses. I used to watch TV, but now I watch horses. Let other people have a view of the ocean – I've got a postcard for a window.

(beat)

When I watch them I wonder what they're thinking. What would you think of if your entire world was reduced to just grass and a blue sky?

TRAVIS. I don't know.

VERONICA. I think that if it was just that, and you didn't know what was coming next, then the only thing you could possibly be is happy.

(beat)

What am I doing here? What am I doing?

TRAVIS. You are a great teacher in a school that is desperate for great teachers.

VERONICA. It's cold and windy and I've got to drive everywhere. People stare at me like I have Spock ears. And I hate country music.

TRAVIS. You'll get used to it.

VERONICA. I don't belong here.

TRAVIS. Everyone loves you.

When I first moved here someone threw a yellow-painted brick through my window. I think it was Heck. But all of these people love you because you're this amazing person.

VERONICA. But I'm not. People need to get that straight –

TRAVIS. I think that they've got you figured out.

VERONICA. No. If they're nice to me it's because you came here first and stuck it out.

TRAVIS. I didn't do anything.

VERONICA. You turned these people from being ignorant bigots into… Well, they're still ignorant, but at least they aren't throwing bricks through our windows.

TRAVIS. If they can't get rid of you then they eventually get used to you.

VERONICA. Did you know that's kind of courageous, Travis?

TRAVIS. I just can't tell when I'm not wanted.

VERONICA. I'm glad that you're here. God, I sound so wack right now.

TRAVIS. Wack?

VERONICA. Bobby Sorenson kept making blow-job hand motions at Elisha Nelson so I sent him to the Principal, and on the way out he very loudly told the class that I was wack –

TRAVIS. You are so not-wack.

VERONICA. I'm glad that I'm not alone.

TRAVIS. Never in your life would you have to worry about something like that.

VERONICA. I don't know how you handled it. Being out here by yourself.

TRAVIS. It doesn't matter where we are. It's just –

(She moves closer.)

VERONICA. It's who's there with us.

TRAVIS. Yeah.

(He kisses her. She yields, but pushes him away.)

VERONICA. We can't, Travis. I'm involved with your friend.

(a short pause)

TRAVIS. Is it because of my friend or because of something else?

VERONICA. What?

TRAVIS. Where is my friend?

(She backs off. No response.)

TRAVIS. All right, I should… I'll go.

(He exits.)

(She straightens the pillows on her couch, and she lies down and closes her eyes.)

Scene Three

(The classroom.)

*(***DEL*** sits in one of the student chairs turning a piece of paper around in his hands.)*

*(***TRAVIS*** enters with his briefcase.)*

DEL. Hi Travis. Um –

TRAVIS. I've got a class starting. What's up.

(He hands **TRAVIS** *the piece of paper.)*

DEL. Read it.

TRAVIS. *(reads)* Something isn't being said. You're keeping something from me… I want you to know that I don't care what it is. What I do care about is that you are keeping secrets from me even though you said that you wouldn't hide… So I want you to tell me… What changed. Because I don't see you much anymore. And I miss you. Love, Veronica.

(beat)

What does this mean? Does she know?

DEL. I don't know.

TRAVIS. Have you been spending less time with her?

DEL. There's a difference between me just coming by at night and me being there all the time.

TRAVIS. Of course there is. You're supposed to be there for her.

DEL. I can't be there all the time. Not the way she wants me.

TRAVIS. You do care about her, don't you?

DEL. Yeah. Course I do. But, I don't know – it's just not the same, me livin' there… I guess… I –

TRAVIS. I understand Del, but it's not that hard if you want to be with her.

DEL. Being there all the time, so close all the time… If she's smiling then everything's all right, but if she's not… Or if it's quiet then… Somebody's gotta say something, right?

TRAVIS. So… What?

DEL. I don't know what to say. What do I say to this?

TRAVIS. I don't know.

DEL. What am I supposed to say when she expects all of these things –

TRAVIS. I don't know –

DEL. That I don't know anything about –

TRAVIS. Well, you're the one that's with her.

(a short pause)

DEL. Please, write her a letter –

TRAVIS. No.

DEL. Just one last time –

TRAVIS. You told me to stop –

DEL. I know I asked you to, but I shouldn't have. I just need you to get me back on track and everything'll be fine –

TRAVIS. *(exasperated)* If you care about her, then write the letters yourself. Tell her –

DEL. Travis, please –

TRAVIS. *(furious)* You're the one she wants, you write the letters –

DEL. I can't do it, okay? I'm stupid and I need your help. Okay? Is that what you want to hear me say? 'cause I don't want to lose her, Travis. You don't know what that's like.

(A bell rings.)

TRAVIS. Go.

*(**DEL** stands there.)*

GO. Please.

*(**DEL** looks back at him, then exits.)*

*(**TRAVIS** opens his briefcase, stares at it, then takes out a book and shuts it.)*

(He takes his seat at the desk.)

Scene Four

(The classroom, later that night.)

(A flashlight in the darkness.)

*(**CHESTER** rummages through the teacher's desk, sliding drawers open and shut, searching for something.)*

(He's dressed as a ninja.)

(There's the click of a lighter. The cherry of a cigarette ignites.)

*(**CHESTER** swings the flashlight around to find **VERONICA** sitting in a student chair, smoking a cigarette.)*

VERONICA. Get the lights.

*(**CHESTER** flicks on the classroom lights.)*

What are you doing in my classroom?

CHESTER. Travis sent me to retrieve his old quizzes for freshman English. Because he's writing a new quiz, you see, and he wants to use the old ones for reference.

VERONICA. What's with the sneaking around?

CHESTER. I'm not sneaking around.

VERONICA. You're dressed like a ninja.

CHESTER. This is what I sleep in.

*(There's a hook sticking out of **CHESTER**'s pants.)*

VERONICA. Is that a grappling hook?

CHESTER. Yes. Why are you smoking a cigarette in your classroom?

VERONICA. I like to do secret things in secret places.

CHESTER. I should go.

VERONICA. You just broke in. Sit.

(He sits.)

VERONICA. So…I know you hate my guts.

CHESTER. No, I – what makes you say that?

(She hands him a letter.)

VERONICA. Read it. Aloud.

CHESTER. *(hesitates, then reads:)* Did I ever tell you that your physical attributes are what get me off the most?

VERONICA. Keep going.

CHESTER. *(reads)* Your silky-straight black hair, your, um, almond-shaped eyes… One of these nights before we get it on, do you think you could serve me some tea? Let us sexualize your traditions, my little dragon –

VERONICA. That's a little out-of-character for Del, wouldn't you say? Does it sound familiar?

CHESTER. No.

VERONICA. Come on, you little Malcolm lower-case x – I saw you slip that into my mailbox!

CHESTER. What do you want me to say? That I forged that letter? That I'm guilty of information warfare? Fine. Guilty.

VERONICA. Be straight with me. Tell me what you really think: Veronica, you are a yellow cab sucking down white semen in an attempt to remove the jaundice from your complexion.

(beat)

I've heard it before. And I don't care if you hate my guts.

CHESTER. I don't hate your guts. I hate the guts of your choices. You choose Del – DEL? He uses the word "dumb" as a noun – "you DUMB!"… And he used to beat me up in Junior High because my parents made me get a crew cut.

VERONICA. You forgot the fact that he's white.

CHESTER. I was just getting to that.

VERONICA. You think that I'm ashamed to be Asian, don't you? How do you think I grew up? Nestled in pink sheets combing the blonde hair of my Barbie dolls? I'm from New York City, pal. So don't think I'm immune to hate. It seeks me out just as much as it does you.

CHESTER. Then what purpose does it serve to slink into The Man's ivory embrace?

VERONICA. Because despite all that, I think that people shouldn't be separated into colors.

CHESTER. Hmmm.

VERONICA. There are only assholes and non-assholes. I choose who I love. And no one will choose for me.

CHESTER. Right. But some colors are better than others, aren't they?

VERONICA. Don't confuse my pride with being ashamed. I'm not ashamed.

CHESTER. So why only white men?

VERONICA. Because that's my choice.

CHESTER. Well, you may have your preferences, and I shall have mine.

VERONICA. And I suppose that your preference is that she be Asian.

CHESTER. Yes.

VERONICA. Why?

CHESTER. Because I have chosen to perpetuate my people. To maintain a strong culture in this outpost of barbarians. But don't think for a second that I want a kow-towing, subservient jade circlet of a wife.

VERONICA. You don't?

CHESTER. No. I want a strong, dynamic Asian Sister. With the rustic beauty of a pony-tailed farm girl off a Maoist propaganda poster. Because I want to find someone that understands me. That shares my skin.

(beat)

But to encounter a Sister like yourself – one that rejects the Asian in the Asian Man… Why, it appalls and bewilders me.

VERONICA. So just because I'm Asian I'm automatically supposed to hook up with an Asian guy? There are only two of you in this town. Doesn't that kind of limit my options?

CHESTER. You haven't even given this little horsie a ride.

VERONICA. You? No way. But keep in mind that I'm not rejecting you based on race.

CHESTER. Well, when you look at me, what do you see?

VERONICA. What?

CHESTER. Do you think that I'm harmless? Do you think that I'm a weak, sniveling pussy that would rather cross the street and push up his glasses instead of confronting trouble?

VERONICA. No.

CHESTER. Then do you think I'm a nerd? A fuckin' FOB-style nerd studying for the GREs in the corner?

VERONICA. You're dressed like a ninja –

CHESTER. Ninjas are fucking cool, lady –

VERONICA. No, I don't think of you as a nerd. Do you think that *I think* that I'm superior to you –

CHESTER. Yes –

VERONICA. Because of who I choose to be with?

CHESTER. Yes – do you think that I'm a misogynist?

VERONICA. Yes.

CHESTER. Do you think I'm effeminate?

VERONICA. No. Do you think I'm a sucky-sucky love-you-long-time leg spreader?

CHESTER. No. Do you think that I'm a racist?

VERONICA. Absolutely – do you think that I would allow myself to be submissive –

CHESTER. Yes –

VERONICA. I'm not finished – that I would stay in a relationship even if I was being mistreated?

CHESTER. …No. So do you think that I'm cold, unemotional –

VERONICA. No; do you think that I'm ashamed of myself?

CHESTER. Why, do you think that I'm ashamed of myself?

VERONICA. I think you are.

CHESTER. Then I think you are. Let's get to the meat: Do you think that I have a small penis?

VERONICA. Yes. Do you think that I want to be white?

CHESTER. Yes.

VERONICA. Do you think that I hate myself?

CHESTER. Yes.

(beat)

Do you think that I hate myself?

VERONICA. Yes.

(a long pause)

CHESTER. And what about Travis?

VERONICA. What about Travis?

CHESTER. I don't care what you think about me. But do you think the same things about him?

VERONICA. I don't know.

CHESTER. What would you do if he made a move on you?

VERONICA. We're friends.

CHESTER. Right. Travis is the friend and Del is the personal rodeo system. Gotcha.

(beat)

You know, you're amazing, lady. You think you're flapping around the heavens on your white winged steed, but...

VERONICA. But what?

CHESTER. I'm just saying, you might not like egg yolks, you avoid 'em as much as possible, but sometimes you just can't help biting into them.

VERONICA. You're weird.

CHESTER. I've been called worse. Especially by your cowboyfriend.

VERONICA. If you're trying to allude to some problems Del and I are having, it's none of your business.

CHESTER. Sure.

VERONICA. But if you know something that you're not telling me –

CHESTER. I know what I know what I know.

VERONICA. And you knowing something that I don't truly sickens me. So spill it.

CHESTER. I have nothing to spill.

VERONICA. How about now?

(She produces the Last Spike, holding it before him like a dagger.)

(His eyes seize upon it, hypnotized –)

I found it locked up in the desk. And I've heard the back story of how it turned up missing at the railroad celebration. "Stolen" is the exact word used. So if someone wants it, all he has to do is spill his guts.

CHESTER. This is a bribe?

VERONICA. I'm either giving it to you or the cops.

CHESTER. And that's all you're offering?

VERONICA. What more do you want?

CHESTER. The spike and a thirty minute make-out session.

VERONICA. You only get the spike.

CHESTER. Lady, do you think that I'd snitch out a Brother? And for what... For a measly spike-shaped piece of gold? These aren't my secrets. They're not mine to give. And that's something you don't know about the Asian Man – something you'll never know. He's Upright. And he doesn't need your gold or anybody else's.

(as he's out the door –)

So you do what you will with that. And if you ever want to see if you're right, call me up. I'll come over and whip it out.

(He exits.)

(fade)

Scene Five

(Outside Travis's house, that night. Sound of traffic on a nearby country road.)

*(***DEL*** is smoking the roach-remains of a joint.)*

*(***TRAVIS*** enters with a bag of groceries, approaches.)*

TRAVIS. Put that out.

DEL. It's almost gone anyway.

TRAVIS. I don't want people seeing some guy smoking weed in front of my house –

DEL. You care what they think. I ain't got that problem.

*(***TRAVIS*** fumbles for his keys, makes a failed attempt to open his front door –)*

I moved back to my dad's ranch. Or at least I tried, 'cause…when I woke up this mornin'… You know that plan I had to put the blame on Bill if my dad caught me smoking weed? Bill thought of it first.

TRAVIS. Are you all right?

DEL. You know my old man. He doesn't like to raise his voice, so all my stuff had already been put in my truck. Secured. No good byes. Just nowhere to go.

(Re: the joint)

Though I managed to steal a consolation prize from Bill.

(He produces a small .38 revolver from his back pocket.)

And a parting gift from dear old Dad.

TRAVIS. Give me that –

*(***TRAVIS*** tries to snatch it, but ***DEL*** pulls it away.)*

DEL. No way, son. If I give it to you now, I won't be able to use it later.

TRAVIS. Goddamn it Del, you give me that gun –

DEL. If you ask nice sometime, I may let you borrow it.

TRAVIS. Where's Veronica?

DEL. Back at her place. She sat me down, told me to write her a letter, right then and there. So I took your advice. I did.

TRAVIS. What did you tell her? You didn't –

DEL. Where did all of it come from, Travis?

TRAVIS. I don't know.

DEL. Man, I am such a *dumb*... I'm such a stupid *dumb*. My balls are cold and empty, and I wanna die.

(beat)

The person you've made us out to be is a lie. He's fiction. And I can't live up to that. What she and I had didn't even match.

(a short pause)

Do you love her?

TRAVIS. I never had a chance with her.

DEL. Fuck that. You love her, you do something about it. If you've got the skills to love her, you use them. Why did you let me take your place?

TRAVIS. Because I never had a chance. She has preferences.

DEL. Whaddaya mean "preferences"?

TRAVIS. You don't get it, do you? She doesn't like men of my persuasion.

DEL. What?

TRAVIS. She doesn't date Asian men.

(A moment as **DEL** *tries to comprehend this –)*

DEL. Why the hell not?

TRAVIS. I don't know.

DEL. That's crazy. You're Ko-rean, she's Ko-rean –

TRAVIS. She's only attracted to white men.

*(***DEL** *tries to comprehend this as well –)*

DEL. Aw, that's horse shit! She loves your letters – it wouldn't matter if you were a chimpanzee. You were just afraid to give 'em to her on your own –

TRAVIS. No. It's because you are my friend. And if you've got a chance and I've got none, I have to give you what I've got.

DEL. But that's not the American Way, Travis. That's, like – I don't even know what that is – but it ain't right.

TRAVIS. Look, you're the one she wanted.

DEL. Why me? Look at me, Travis! I've been wearing these same pants for three years. I won this hat in a contest. My dad keeps a collection of priceless gold coins and I steal his cheap motherfuckin' gun?

TRAVIS. Yeah, look at you. You're all rippled and blonde, and everyone wants a piece of apple pie –

DEL. Without you I wouldn't have had a chance with Veronica.

TRAVIS. But the ladies sure do love the cowboys.

DEL. I'm not a real cowboy, Travis. Let's get that straight right now. The real cowboys are dead. All that's left is dude ranches and souvenir belt buckles. This ain't about cowboys. This is about you feeling sorry and scared for yourself. And I don't like having cowards as friends.

TRAVIS. I'm a coward? Look, you had me write the letters for you because you couldn't get up the nerve –

DEL. I haven't spent the last few years hiding in a little shit-hole town where I don't belong! For what? 'cause you can't own up to yourself –

TRAVIS. It was my choice to come here. I decided to start over –

DEL. Starting over means beginning a brand new life. But you won't do that – you refuse to take any chance that comes to you –

TRAVIS. What do you want me to do?

DEL. Speak for yourself. But you won't. Because you ran away from your own life. You came here to die.

(a short pause)

TRAVIS. Does she know who really writes the letters?

DEL. Do what you shoulda done and ask her yourself.

*(**DEL** re-lights the joint, takes a drag.)*

TRAVIS. What are you going to do with the gun?

DEL. Drive back to my dad's ranch and kill everyone I see.

(beat)

I'm just kidding, man. I'll probably sell it at a pawn shop. I wasn't gonna do nothing with it. It ain't even loaded –

*(The gun goes off in **DEL**'s hand – he drops it, and both of them leap out of their skins –)*

TRAVIS & DEL. JESUS CHRIST!

(A pause as they check themselves for bullet holes – they're intact.)

DEL. You shot?

TRAVIS. No, are you?

DEL. I'm all right, I think. Ow... What'd I tell you, Travis? I ain't no cowboy.

*(**DEL** offers the joint to **TRAVIS**, who declines.)*

*(**TRAVIS** gingerly picks up the gun.)*

TRAVIS. Come inside. You can stay with me.

DEL. I was hoping you'd say that.

TRAVIS. You think she'll be mad?

DEL. Yeah. But she probably won't stay that way forever. After all, she didn't want another cowboy, Travis. She wanted you.

(They stare at each other as the sound of traffic slowly fades to silence.)

Scene Six

(The classroom, the next day.)

*(***VERONICA*** hastily packs her things into a cardboard box.)*

*(***TRAVIS*** watches her from the doorway –)*

TRAVIS. Grady says that he wants to give you your own classroom. So I take it you're moving your things there?

VERONICA. *(cold)* No, Travis, I'm not.

(an awkward pause)

TRAVIS. So you know who really writes you the letters.

VERONICA. Your scumbag friend ratted you out.

TRAVIS. Chester?

VERONICA. No. Del.

(beat)

See, that's courage, Travis. You could learn a lot from him. He popped his head out of his little rat hole even though a lawn mower was about to run right over it –

TRAVIS. Veronica –

VERONICA. You lied to me –

TRAVIS. I meant everything that I said to you in those letters –

VERONICA. With the exception of Del's signature at the bottom. You scared me into thinking that he couldn't fully open up to me. He had to write me letters to communicate?

TRAVIS. Oh God –

VERONICA. You made me question myself and our relationship, and in the end the whole thing turned out to be a gigantic lie.

TRAVIS. What was I supposed to do?

VERONICA. You were supposed to sign the letters, "Love, Travis."

TRAVIS. Yeah, well, you have preferences.

VERONICA. What the hell is that supposed to mean?

TRAVIS. Oh come on, Ms. When-The-Right-Man-Comes-Along – let me rephrase that – Ms. When-The-White-Man-Comes-Along!

VERONICA. Fuck you, Travis – you know I'm not like that –

TRAVIS. Sure. You're all set on being alone but shazam – along comes Del with his Ford F-150 –

VERONICA. You're ridiculous, you know that?

TRAVIS. Yeah, you think you've got a Genuine Cowboy, but oops, out pops a guy with chopsticks.

VERONICA. Yes, it's all my fault for thinking I was in a relationship with one great guy when, in reality, I was in a relationship with two dumbs –

TRAVIS. You wanted it all – all the poetry and romance combined with Mister steak-eating America –

VERONICA. And you were full of shit when you said that you didn't care. When you found out that I was attracted to white men it cut your dick off. And you decided to punish me –

TRAVIS. Hah –

VERONICA. Because of who I am –

TRAVIS. Then tell me what it means when a woman who is so afraid of being fetishized by the American porno industry declares that you are only attracted to – I mean, you only fetishize – white men. Isn't that just slightly hypocritical?

VERONICA. What?

TRAVIS. You heard me.

VERONICA. If I were you I wouldn't bring up Asian fetish porn.

TRAVIS. Why is that?

VERONICA. Because I've been to your house. And your underwear drawer isn't something that I'd show to your mother.

TRAVIS. Why, you…

VERONICA. That's right, I located it: "Oriental Lesbo Sluts #3"? "Spankable Japanese Panty-Nurses"? "FAR EAST FUCK FEST"?!

TRAVIS. It's not like porno companies produce non-Asian-Fetish porn! If I wanna see naked Asian women, I don't have a choice!

VERONICA. So do you think that you're being a racist when you buy that garbage?

TRAVIS. No. When I buy that garbage I'm being horny.

VERONICA. So you have aesthetic tastes and needs. And so did I. Del is sweet and simple, but that by itself isn't enough. By reading his letters he was showing me who he was. But when I found out that they weren't from him, my love for him fell apart. I let him down. And the love he was giving me was all fiction. You let me down.

TRAVIS. I didn't mean to.

VERONICA. And neither did he. But the two of you never figured it out. It wasn't about his skin. It was about how you made me feel. Because for a moment... For quite a few moments, you made me feel good. Was it real?

TRAVIS. You let me know from the start that you have preferences –

VERONICA. Then fuck the preferences.

(beat)

But even then, you're still ashamed of who you are.

TRAVIS. No, I'm not.

VERONICA. Then what about Grace?

TRAVIS. What about her?

VERONICA. You let me think that she was Asian, but she wasn't. Grace Thompson. There is a shoebox in your closet full of pictures, wedding invitations. And Del told me the rest –

TRAVIS. That –

VERONICA. Her father said that if she went ahead and married you, her family would not be present at the ceremony. And so it never happened. And so here you are.

TRAVIS. That wasn't her fault.

VERONICA. But do you think that it was yours? And when are you planning on letting that go?

*(**TRAVIS** is silent now.)*

By the way, this belongs to your friend.

(She puts the Last Spike on the desk.)

I tried to bribe him with it, but the little creep wouldn't take it. That's courage.

(She heads toward the door.)

TRAVIS. Veronica, I'm –

VERONICA. I know you are. But it doesn't matter much anymore.

*(She exits. **TRAVIS** watches her go.)*

(He walks over to his desk, unlocks a drawer.)

(He is about to put the spike in, but stops.)

(He sits at the desk, holding the spike in his hands.)

Scene Seven

(Outdoors. A slow, warm spotlight comes up on **DEL** *wearing a baseball glove. He pitches out an invisible ball.)*

(Another slow, warm spotlight comes up on **TRAVIS** *on the opposite side, also wearing a baseball glove. He catches the ball.)*

(The game of catch continues.)

DEL. Have you met TJ?

TRAVIS. He's your replacement, right?

DEL. Yeah. He's from Great Falls. Man, he's a professional. He brought a uniform to teach in and everything.

TRAVIS. The kids are going to miss you.

DEL. Me? Naw. They'll be all right. Though I am going to miss throwin' dodgeballs at 'em. That was a perk.

TRAVIS. Are you sure you want to move to L.A.?

DEL. It's Hollywood, Travis. I'm going to Hollywood.

TRAVIS. Hollywood is pretty much in L.A.

DEL. It is? Goddamn. They should let people know that.

(beat)

Man, I wanna see palm trees and cars with hydraulic bumping action. I'm gonna learn to surf. I wanna get lost.

(beat)

And I know it's an easy out with Veronica, but I figure it's for the best… Hey – remember that letter you wrote to her about Blue?

TRAVIS. Your horse?

DEL. Oh man, you got that all wrong. I hated that fucking horse.

TRAVIS. What?

DEL. He was a mean son of a bitch. We had this theory that he started the fire in stable.

TRAVIS. Horses don't start fires.

DEL. This one did! He'd do anything to escape. He was straight-loco. The night of the fire we let out the horses, and yeah – Blue burst out burning. But instead of lying down to die, he took off like a bolt. A fireball, man. And we never found his body.

TRAVIS. Really?

DEL. Yeah. He got away clean, one way or the other. And I always thought, "Good for him."

(a short pause)

TRAVIS. It's gonna be hard starting over by yourself.

DEL. Don't worry about me, Travis. I got a roommate.

*(**CHESTER** enters carrying a box filled with various Asian goods –)*

CHESTER. Can we stop by my parents' place? I need to pick up my zither.

TRAVIS. Now this I can't believe. You're moving in with Captain Rice over here?

DEL. It'll be nice to know someone from my home town, even if he does have controversial beliefs. And if he gets to worryin' me I'll give him a poke in the eye.

CHESTER. And I'll do anything to escape from Randall and Betty's basement. I will miss Betty's apple turnovers, but she is willing to FedEx them.

TRAVIS. Where'd you find the money to leave?

CHESTER. I sold everything I own, including a few stolen cases of Fire Sauce culled from Taco Tuesday. Survivalists, Travis. They'll buy anything in bulk. And it's all worth it – I'm gonna inject myself into an enormous Asian female population.

TRAVIS. If you do, try to keep the hard-core militancy down to a low rumble.

CHESTER. Of course. I plan to bring the honey when I tempt the baby bees.

TRAVIS. *(amused)* It sounds like Chester A. Arthur is finally growing up.

CHESTER. PLEASE: Don't call me by my full name.

DEL. He doesn't like that.

CHESTER. Oh, and by the way – about –

TRAVIS. The Last Spike?

CHESTER. Yeah – did you –

TRAVIS. Well, Hallsey's been sniffing around but he hasn't been able to connect it to us.

CHESTER. Great. So can I have my spike back –

TRAVIS. NO. I got rid of it.

CHESTER. What?

TRAVIS. I walked along the railroad tracks until I forgot where I was. Then I dug a hole and buried it. I don't think that even I could find it again if I tried.

CHESTER. I see.

TRAVIS. I'm glad that you do.

CHESTER. Travis, before I depart, I wanted to say that... I never knew what brotherhood was until I met you. Before you arrived, I was an only child.

TRAVIS. That's probably the most touching, least-offensive thing I've ever heard you say.

CHESTER. Well, we Vietnamese know the importance of family.

*(**TRAVIS** and **CHESTER** shake hands.)*

DEL. Come with us.

TRAVIS. I can't.

DEL. Come on, Travis. You got nothing left for you here. Heck's gonna close up the bar and become a greeter at Wal-Mart. And Shelby's going under because of the Albertson's in Cheyenne. Everyone's taking off.

TRAVIS. Well, I'm staying. I like it. I can finally sleep.

DEL. All right, Travis.

*(nods to **CHESTER**)*

You wanna get on?

CHESTER. Yeah. I wanna see an ocean.

(to **TRAVIS***)*

Stay strong, my Brother.

DEL. So long, cowboy.

*(***DEL** *and* **CHESTER** *exit.)*

*(***TRAVIS** *squeezes his baseball glove, handles the invisible ball in its palm.)*

(He tosses it way up into the air and catches it.)

(He repeats, playing catch by himself in slow, lonely turns.)

(fade)

Scene Eight

(The classroom, the next day.)

*(***VERONICA*** sits at the teacher's desk.)*

(Across its surface are piles of scratcher tickets. She scratches them off one by one.)

*(***TRAVIS*** enters, surprised to see her.)*

(She quickly begins to gather up the tickets.)

VERONICA. I know all of my things are supposed to be out of your room, but – I'll be gone in a second –

TRAVIS. No, it's okay.

(Re: the scratcher tickets)

I thought you just collect them.

VERONICA. Yeah, well… I thought I could stand to open myself up to a little disappointment.

TRAVIS. Did you win anything?

VERONICA. Seven years ago I won fifty thousand dollars.

TRAVIS. You're kidding.

(She hands him a scratcher ticket.)

(reads) "Happiness."

VERONICA. Do you think I should be upset?

TRAVIS. It depends on whether you think fifty thousand dollars is a lot of money.

VERONICA. I could've used it seven years ago.

TRAVIS. And now?

VERONICA. There are more important things, don't you think?

(A short pause. She gathers up the scratcher tickets.)

TRAVIS. You know, I walked to school today along the highway. I hadn't done that since I first got here. I walked past Dr. Peters' place –

VERONICA. Travis –

TRAVIS. Looking for you. I looked through the window of your cottage, saw that the place was empty – nothing left, not even a jar with a dead animal floating in it –

VERONICA. Travis, please…

TRAVIS. I was looking for you because –

VERONICA. Maggie's driving me to Jackson. I've got a flight to catch.

TRAVIS. I wanted to give you this.

(He produces a sealed envelope.)

VERONICA. So what does it say?

(He holds it up, still sealed –)

TRAVIS. It says that… It's strange how we can become whatever we want on paper.

It says that it's a powerful thing, the closest thing we have in the world to real magic.

That when you write something down, you become words, you shed everything that you really are. And I was ready to become whatever you wanted in order to earn your love. Because you collect scratcher tickets. Because you came two thousand miles to just try it out. Because you're funny, and you're beautiful, and you're a nerd.

And it says that I'm sorry that I was afraid to love you, and that I'm not afraid anymore.

Because all these things that you are, Veronica: They are greater than the sum of my fears.

And then it says my signature at the bottom.

(He offers it to her.)

VERONICA. I can't.

TRAVIS. Why not?

VERONICA. Being loved on paper is not enough. I need to learn how to love someone in person. And so do you.

TRAVIS. Maybe we can learn to do that together.

VERONICA. I'll tell you what, Travis: I'll make you a deal. Give me some time. Take some time for yourself. And then you come find me.

TRAVIS. Veronica –

VERONICA. When you're ready, you come find me. I won't hide.

(She produces a stack of letters bound by a string. She places it on the desk.)

TRAVIS. No – I want you to keep them.

VERONICA. But they're yours. Hold on to them. Look them over, see who you really are.

(After a pause, he accepts the letters.)

(She takes her things and exits.)

*(**TRAVIS** stares at the closed door, paces. He looks at the stack of letters in his hand.)*

(He tears off the string, quickly scans the first letter and throws it on the ground.)

(He looks over another letter, throws it away, he tosses all of the letters into the air.)

*(They float downward in a cloud, and **TRAVIS** looks up at them as if lost in a storm.)*

(And he rushes over to the door, opens it to go after her –)

*(But **VERONICA** is standing there behind it, her back turned, apparently trying to convince herself to walk away.)*

(They are surprised to see each other. He smiles. And she does as well. She holds the door open for him.)

(And he exits with her, closing the door behind him.)

(fade)

End of Act Two

End of Play

ABOUT THE PLAYWRIGHT

Michael Golamco is an LA-based playwright and screenwriter. The New York premiere of his play *Year Zero* opened at Second Stage in May 2010. It previously received an acclaimed run at the Victory Gardens Theatre in Chicago and was the Grand Prize Winner of Chicago Dramatists' Many Voices Project. His play *Cowboy Versus Samurai* has had several productions since its premiere in NYC, including in Canada and Hong Kong. Michael is the recipient of the 2009 Helen Merrill Award and is a member of New Dramatists. He is currently working on new play commissions for South Coast Repertory and Second Stage Theatre.

As a screenwriter, Michael's film *Please Stand By* was presented at the 2009 Tribeca Film Festival's On Track film development program. His short film, *Dragon of Love,* was awarded Best Short Film at the Hawaii International Film Festival and ran in regular rotation on the Sundance Channel.

OTHER TITLES AVAILABLE FROM SAMUEL FRENCH

YEAR ZERO

Michael Golamco

Dramatic Comedy / 3m, 1f

Vuthy Vichea is sixteen years old, Cambodian American. He loves hip hop and Dungeons and Dragons. He has thick-ass glasses. He is a weird kid in a place where weirdness can be fatal: Long Beach, California. Since his best friend moved and his mother died, the only person he can talk to is a human skull he keeps hidden in a cookie jar. *Year Zero* is a comedic drama about young Cambodian Americans — about reincarnation, reinvention, and ultimately, redemption.

"[A] tenderly observed play… These characters are cut from familiar molds, but Mr. Golamco and his appealing cast bring fresh nuances, tempering the earnestness with unassuming charm."
– *New York Times*

"A very smart, sweet, honest and uncommonly moving new play… Michael Golamco is a significant new dramatic voice."
– *Chicago Tribune*

"A delicate portrait of lost souls attempting to discover their roots and navigate awkward relationships with one another… Incisive, both dramatically and thematically, leading to a haunting and hopeful climax. Critic's Pick!"
– *Backstage*

CPSIA information can be obtained
at www.ICGtesting.com
Printed in the USA
LVHW012300240723
753342LV00007B/239